MANDI RICHARDS

FALCON'S KISS

PRINCESSES OF SELMY ISLAND BOOK 1

FALCON'S KISS

First edition. November 22, 2022.

ISBN: 979-8215255490

Written by Mandi Richards.

This book is dedicated to my favorite friend for introducing me to the fantasy genre, turning me into an instant addict, and to my mom for letting me read her paperback romances when I was a teenager.

I

Marya

Her mother used to tell her she could do anything she dreamed of doing. What her mother had meant was that she could marry any man she wanted to and be whatever type of wife he needed her to be.

At least, that is what she was coming to realize as she sat in her first council meeting after her parents' death. Her mother and father had only passed a few hours ago, and Marya Sova and her brother Ivan had been dragged into a meeting with their father's political advisers. Well, Ivan had been dragged in. Marya had insisted on being included, much to the annoyance of her father's councilors—No, Ivan's councilors now.

She had only been in the council chambers occasionally. Her father had let her accompany him for much of his work, but he had drawn the line at attending council meetings. Even Ivan had been excluded from most meetings. At eight and twenty, her brother had been old enough to have trained with their father. Showing no inclination towards politics, her father had not forced the issue. Now it was too late.

Marya took in the room around her. It was stuffy and warm, and she had expected it to be grander. As far as kings went, her father's tastes had been simple. At least, she imagined so, having visited no other kingdoms before. They sat around a large oak table. Ivan sat in the center of the long end, with Marya to his right. On his left sat Uncle Tavar, her father's chief adviser. Opposite them sat eight other men, all graying, and all shooting annoyed looks in her direction. It was as if her very presence offended them.

Marya ignored them. She held her head high and tried to listen to what everyone said. Processing what was going on was difficult when she wished to throw herself down on her bed and cry or run through the forest as fast as she could until she could no longer think. She needed to pay attention if she wanted to help Ivan keep their kingdom running.

She watched her brother closely. She had chosen the seat beside him to make a point, but it was difficult to make out his expression from that angle. He had run his hands through his short, deep-brown hair repeatedly until it stood on end. His wide-eyed expression was akin to an owl confronted with the bright light of day. Throughout the meeting, he blinked rapidly in a dazed sort of manner, as if he could not believe what they said. Marya wondered if the other men had noticed the comparison, with the large tapestry of their family's crest, a snowy owl behind him.

The owl tapestry was one of the few decorations adorning the stone walls, lending credence to Marya's theory about her father's simple tastes.

An awkward silence descended on the room. Marya had missed what Tavar had said. She had been about to ask when finally, Ivan spoke. "I need more time," he begged.

"Unfortunately, we do not have more time," Tavar responded. "Our island would be an asset to any kingdom. Our trading partners are envious of us. Our copper deposits are valuable. We have very profitable trade deals with all the neighboring kingdoms for our copper. Avoiding the trading costs and gaining direct access to our mines would be advantageous to any kingdom—Not to mention how popular our winterberry crop has been in Wendyl. We also grow and sell a plethora of root vegetables, especially to Azria."

"But none of that has changed," Marya said. "Father and I talked at length about our trade deals with other kingdoms. They were more than fair for all involved. Why should that change just because Ivan is the new king?"

"I will never understand why your father saw fit to teach you about our foreign relations. But if you must know, I suspect that the other kingdoms maintained peace with us because our small island kingdom was not worth the fight. Your father commanded a strong naval force to protect the kingdom. If we show any sign of weakness, other kingdoms may see it as an easy opportunity to annex a prosperous island as part of their kingdom."

Marya thought this through. Their small kingdom was an island situated between two large continents—Dudaimash to their west and Torraellium to their east. They had always had amicable trade agreements with the nearby kingdoms of Azria, Wendyl, and Southshore on the surrounding continents. She did not understand why the kingdoms would suddenly make war over trade agreements.

"Would they try to invade now, just because Father is gone?" Marya asked.

"The King of Wendyl is the only remaining full blooded fae on our continent. They do not call him 'The Warrior King' for nothing. When the Fae Gates first closed, with him in the human realm instead of the fae realm, he terrified a group of bandits into serving him and used them to conquer all the land that he now calls his kingdom," Tavar explained. "He still commands a powerful army. It's true much time has passed since the days of his glorious conquest, but our tiny kingdom might look like an easy enough target to release the warrior once more."

Marya rolled her eyes. "King Nasir may command a great army, but his navy is no match for ours."

She noticed a very mixed reaction to her knowledge of foreign policy. Most of the councilors looked annoyed with her for even considering offering her opinions. Ivan, however, relaxed, knowing she had things in hand. Uncle Tavar's reaction was the hardest to comprehend. He looked at her, almost wistfully. Marya wondered if he was thinking of her father, his step-brother and close companion, when he heard her talk. She resembled him physically, with her dark hair and brows. She would be proud to be like him in other ways too.

"Young Lady," a councilor, an older man with white hair and a close-cropped beard, addressed her. "While your father may have taught you a thing or two about our neighbors, I hardly think you are qualified to say what their intentions are or are not regarding our kingdom."

Marya balled her hands into fists, suddenly glad for the heavy table between them.

"Besides," the white-haired councilor continued in his condescending tone, "You are forgetting about Azria. Their desert kingdom is practically barren. They get the majority of their food crops from surrounding kingdoms. It is very costly to import so much with very little to export in return. Cutting out the middleman from some of their trades would be a smart move for them."

"Yes," Tavar agreed. "Lord Digby is correct. Azria is likely the biggest threat. They are a very private kingdom, and we know little about their king, but their kingdom has always been jealous of their more prosperous neighbors."

Marya was unsure what to think. It seemed audacious that these kings would jump to take over their small island, just because of a change in ruler. Could Selmy really be that valuable an asset? Uncle Tavar had been their father's most trusted advisor. If father had trusted him so wholeheartedly, she would have to put her faith in him. If he said it was so, she would have to believe it.

Ivan did not have a strong enough personality for the job. He wasn't inspiring the way her father had been. He knew nothing about commanding Father's naval fleet, or even the day to day running of the kingdom. And it meant they were doomed.

"Surely, we have just a little more time." Ivan raked his messy brown hair back from his forehead yet again. She could see the panic returning to his eyes.

"Your coronation will be in three days' time. Your parents let you grow soft, spending all your time reading and studying. I sure hope you read some books on foreign policy, and how to run a kingdom. I will not stand by and watch this kingdom fall apart." Marya had rarely heard Uncle Tavar so passionate. However, she had never seen him in a council meeting before. No one else seemed surprised, and the other councilors nodded in agreement.

Tavar was right about Ivan, but he did not need to be so harsh. Everyone knew Ivan would be no comparison to her father, but to call him out for it so publicly. Tavar and the others would just have to find ways to help him. He would figure it after some time—she hoped.

It was unfair that she had been born female. She may not know everything her father had, but she knew more than Ivan. And she would be eager to learn, unlike Ivan, who had no interest. So what if she was a woman? Why couldn't she be in charge?

"I'll do it!" Marya spoke up at last.

"You'll do what?" Tavar asked.

"I'll rule the kingdom. I'm eldest, and I have paid attention to what father does—did." she corrected herself, swallowing down the lump that formed in her throat.

"You know that cannot happen," Lord Digby spoke up. Lord Digby was getting on her nerves. He was a stubborn old man who had been on the king's council long before her father was king.

"And why not?" she asked. "There are kingdoms with female rulers."

"Not Selmy," Lord Digby responded.

"Well then, let us do it together. Ivan can be the king in name, but I will assist him." Honestly, she was not sure she wanted to be queen, anyway. She just wanted to make sure the job was done right, and she really would enjoy helping him. It could give her a sense of purpose. There was very little for a princess to do in a kingdom, and Marya was used to making the decisions among her siblings. Why should running the kingdom be any different?

"I spent the last several years watching and learning from Father," she explained. "I know how to do it all. And I've spent more time out in the city than anyone. I've even toured the countryside with father, checking in with farmers and winemakers and artisans. I know what our people need. Put me on the council, at least. I can teach Ivan." Marya had loved her trips into the city of Oolaiah and the surrounding countryside with her father. She never understood why Ivan didn't want to go with them.

"No, Marya," Ivan spoke up. He looked at her, his emerald green eyes meeting her identical ones in a firm stare. "That will never work because you will need to marry and move to your own household. You will be too busy with your obligations as a wife."

"What?" Marya asked, her voice coming out in a shrill whine that she had not meant to use. It was the last thing she had expected him to say! Ivan had never cared for those things before. "I think we have more important things to worry about than finding me a husband."

"No. It is important. You cannot stay here and fix all my problems. If we do not hurry, you will be too old. And once we've found you a husband, we can find suitable matches for Olga and Anna."

"Ivan, where is this coming from?" she asked. He knew she had no interest in marriage. Oola only knew it would be easy to find her a suitable husband if she wanted one. There was plenty of money for her dowry. And marrying into the royal family was an honor that any of Selmy's nobility would have sought after, even the surrounding kingdoms' nobility as well. She was sure.

While she would never be one of the genuine beauties that had men swooning as they walked by, she knew she was attractive. Like all her siblings, she had inherited her mother's high cheekbones and green eyes. And she had her father's thick brown locks, so dark as to be almost black, just like Ivan. If she had wanted a husband, she would have had one already. Surely Ivan understood that. What was he playing at?

"Your brother is right, Marya," Tavar commented. "It's the first decent idea he has had. We could use it to our advantage, to strengthen our political ties with the other kingdoms. If we had powerful allies, it wouldn't matter as much if we didn't have a powerful ruler ourselves. Perhaps we could find alliances with all three of you, lovely ladies."

Ivan winced. She could tell how he felt. She felt embarrassed for both of them. It was common knowledge that he was not keen to rule, but it was another thing for Uncle Tavar to call him out about his lack of ideas in a council meeting. Her uncle acted like she and her sisters were just some bargaining chips to secure friends and ward off enemies.

"Do we have time to invite emissaries from other kingdoms to the coronation?" chimed in another councilor, whose name Marya could not remember. Probably another Digby. The Digby family was essential to the kingdom. They made up a vast majority of the courtiers with whom she was acquainted. "We will begin looking for a proper husband at the coronation ball."

"Wait! Who said I want to marry at all?" she spat.

"Of course, you want to be married," replied the first, older Lord Digby. "All young ladies want to find a husband."

Marya almost groaned out loud. He would think that. The Digbys were famous for their prolific lineage. He had something like seventeen grandchildren. Marya took a deep breath, trying to prevent herself from causing a scene. Heat crept up her neck, and a familiar itching sensation inched down her legs. She wanted to scream. Or run. She needed to run. It was the only thing that would calm her down, and she needed to keep her calm if she would convince them to let her be anything more than some foreign nobleman's wife.

"Not this young lady," she forced out through gritted teeth. She needed to leave before she said something she would regret later. Marya stood from her chair. As calmly as she could manage, she slowly exited the room. Not one of the men in the room made any attempt to stop her. She waited until the door had closed behind her. Then she ran.

Marya had not dressed for running. She usually ran first thing in the morning in simple dresses. She had begged her mother for something that allowed her to run without a corset. She would return from her run for a bath and change into her proper princess attire before the rest of her siblings got out of bed. It was harder to breathe her current restrictive garment, and her fashionable slippers had no traction on the smooth marble floors. At least she had worn a skirt that flared away from her legs with hoops instead of the layers of frilly fabric that some petticoats required that that would tangle her legs.

She slowed her pace a bit to prevent further slipping, but the moment she noticed the rougher terrain of the path under her feet, she took off like the wind. She was Otreus-Blessed. His Divine Gift of speed, let her run faster than any human should be capable of running. She loved to run, but what a useless Gift for a princess. It was not as if she needed to outrun anyone in the palace.

Perhaps she could run away from all her suitors. She laughed at the thought, gasping a bit for breath in her tight corset.

She ran down the gravel path, through the gardens, past the greenhouses, until she reached the forest. She was still on her family's land, and it was not a dangerous forest. The groundskeepers kept it stocked with appropriate wildlife for the pampered boys who frequented the palace to go out in for hunts. It helped them feel tough while putting no one in danger.

Marya liked the forest, too. It gave her solace without upsetting her parents. A pang of sadness again shot through her at the thought of her parents. She faltered slightly in her running, but she pushed on.

She enjoyed the challenge of weaving between the trees and jumping over roots. She liked the way the light shone through the trees as she ran. The gentle flickering helped to calm her mind and her body. She wondered, however, what it would be like to run in a straight, smooth line somewhere open? No such place existed on the palace grounds. She would like to test how fast she could go.

Eventually, Marya stopped, in a familiar clearing, contemplating everything that had happened since that morning.

Her parents' death had not been a surprise, but it still hurt knowing that her mother and father were gone. It was not the all-encompassing, heart-wrenching grief she had feared it would. It was more like a toothache, only in her soul. It did not hurt too badly unless she prodded at it.

They had been loving parents. They trained their four children in their various responsibilities as members of the royal family but gave them the freedom to be who they wanted to be.

That was what had gotten them into this mess. Mother and Father had given Ivan leave to spend all of his time reading and studying. They allowed Marya to follow Father around in his duties. Her younger sisters seemed to fall more naturally into their roles as princesses.

Her youngest sister, Anna, was a starry-eyed dreamer. She was everyone's favorite—sweet and funny. She enjoyed playing tricks, but they were harmless and usually made everyone laugh. It offered the opportunity for everyone to say how cute and clever she was. She would have no problems marrying when the time came. She was probably already planning the day.

And Olga, her middle sister, well Marya was unsure what Olga liked. She was hard to read. She always did as she was told, and she tried to keep the peace between the rest of the siblings. When her turn came to find a husband, she would likely smile and accept her responsibility. No one would be any wiser as to whether or not it was what she wanted.

Why, then, was it so hard for Marya to accept her fate? She should have known it was coming. But, somehow, it had always seemed like she had some other purpose. She was not meant to be some nobleman's wife. She was the only one with the sense to keep their kingdom afloat. Marya was used to doing everything for herself.

How could she have been so stupid? That would never work. It just wasn't the way of things. Being forced to marry might be a blessing. She might wed a lesser noble with a lackluster personality who would let her have control over his estate. It was possible, even, that she might marry some prince from a faraway land where a woman's intelligence was appreciated.

They would go on a grand adventure to reach his palace, and he would come to see her as an asset to his kingdom. She would be more than just her title, and he would make her his equal. Marya snorted. She sounded as foolish as Anna. Men like that did not exist. If she ever married, she wanted it to be her choice, not because her uncle and her brother forced her, and certainly not because they thought there was no other way she could help.

She needed to calm down. She would need to compose herself before she returned. She would march back into the council room and rationally explain how she could help Selmy Island.

Marya lay down on the grass and closed her eyes. She knew she must look ridiculous with the hoops of her skirt pushed up allowing anyone to see her undergarments. Good thing no one else was likely to be in the forest.

Taking deep breaths, she listened to the sounds of the surrounding forest. The leaves rustled. Birds chirped. She heard slight crunching noises of small animals scurrying about their day. Placing one hand on her chest and the other on her abdomen, she breathed in as deeply as her corset would allow.

Breathe in.

Breathe out.

In and out. Slowly, she breathed, tuning out her surroundings until she could feel the itching fade. Keeping her eyes closed, Marya pushed herself up. While concentrating on her breathing, she stretched her arms, then her legs. She opened her eyes and looked around.

The chittering of the forest animals returned to her. A falcon sat on a branch, watching her. Why would a falcon be watching her? It was probably just her imagination. Though she saw nothing else for him to look at. The clearing was empty, except for the two of them. Perhaps it was a good omen. Her Gift of speed was from the god Otreus, the Falcon Prince, after all. Had he sent her a messenger to guide her?

The falcon stared at her a moment longer. Then he blinked a few times and alighted from the branch, up into the skies. What freedom! Marya imagined a world where she could go anywhere she pleased. She knew it wasn't realistic. They all had their roles in life to fulfill. And hers, it seemed, would be to marry some stuffy nobleman. She only hoped it would be someone who would appreciate her for who she was.

"Maaarya," a voice interrupted her daydreaming. "Maryaaaaaa."

How long had she been in the forest? It could not have been that long.

"Over here," she called. Her two sisters popped into the clearing.

"Where have you been?" asked Olga.

"I just went for a run."

"I don't like to use my Gift on you, Marya," Anna said, "But I barely need it to feel your erratic flow of emotions. I understand the sadness, but why are you angry, and confused?"

Marya replayed her conversation with Ivan and his councilors for her sisters.

"Well, that's not so bad," Anna replied. "Imagine! A ball all to find you a husband! That sounds exciting. Like something out of a story."

"But I do not want to marry anyone. And certainly not someone from another kingdom. I want to stay here, and help Ivan get settled into his role."

"Ivan will be fine," Anna replied.

Olga didn't appear convinced. As usual, she held her tongue, refusing to show any opinion of her own.

"I am not so sure about that. You should have seen him at the council meeting. He barely said a word until his absurd proclamation about needing to find a husband for me."

"You will make a beautiful bride," Anne crooned. "Oh, please find a husband quickly, so I can have my turn." She linked her arms with Marya and started back towards the palace.

"Why are you so eager to find a husband?" Olga asked, following along beside them.

"It just seems so magical. I want to wear a beautiful dress embroidered with lilacs and a long train. And we could get married in the spring, out in the gardens."

Marya and Olga chuckled.

"That sounds lovely, Anna. I had not thought of marriage at all," Olga replied. "I suppose if it helps our kingdom, I will have to make a go of it, though."

Marya almost laughed out loud. Her sisters' thoughts on marriage were precisely as she had guessed. Aside from wanting to help Ivan, she also did not wish to leave her family. She had no memories from the time before she had her brother and sisters. Life without Anna's infectious charm or Olga's calming presence was unfathomable. She would even miss Ivan's brooding.

II

Ferrand

"Well, what did she see?"

Prince Ferrand Faucon sat in a grand wooden chair in his father's opulent office. His father, the King of Southshore, was waiting for his report. For days, his falcon familiar, Geraldine, had been flying around Selmy Castle, waiting for the death of King and Queen Sova. That morning, their time had come.

Ferrand hesitated in answering his father. He had not wanted to spy on the family, but his father had insisted on using the telepathic link between Geri and himself to find out information on the new king. What could he tell his father? The Sovas were a family in mourning. It was none of his, or his father's, business what they were up to. He knew his father would be pleased to hear about the new king's apparent lack of leadership skills.

He could not understand why his father obsessed over the tiny kingdom. They had a decent trade agreement on copper, and the kingdom did not have any other resources that Southshore needed. Southshore was already the wealthiest kingdom in Torraellium. It was a waste of time to worry about Selmy Island.

His father's deep brown eyes stared at him from the other side of his enormous mahogany desk, waiting for a reply. With their fae heritage, his father's age did not show. Other than the permanent scowl on his father's face, and his short-cropped hair, Ferrand could have been looking in a mirror. They shared deep blue eyes, flawless golden-brown skin, and jet black hair. Ferrand enjoyed the feel of the wind in his shoulder length locks when he sailed his ship too much to cut it. It was just one more thing to stoke his father's dissaproval.

His father gestured impatiently.

"There was nothing much to see," he said. "They are deeply grieving their losses. The king's councilors met to discuss arrangements for his coronation ceremony. Though, I am sure you will hear of that in due time. They plan to invite the nobility from the nearby kingdoms to attend."

"A wise move. They will need to strengthen their alliances," his father responded. "Perhaps the young king is wiser that I had suspected." Ferrand did not have the heart to tell his father that Ivan Sova had barely said a word during the entire meeting, and his advisors had made all the pertinent decisions. However, Sova had been the one to suggest his sister marry; it was the only thing he seemed to have an opinion about.

"Is that all?" His father asked.

"They plan to use the coronation ball as a chance to search for a suitable marriage candidate for the oldest princess," Ferrand continued, unsure what information his father wanted.

"A husband, you say? Yes. That is excellent news."

"I confess, Father, I do not understand your sudden interest in the small island kingdom. We are on solid terms with them, and they have nothing that we need."

"Ferrand, my son. I think it is time we find you a wife," his father responded, without answering his question. It seemed like a complete change of subject until Ferrand realized he meant the Sova Princess. His stomach turned to lead at the thought.

"You cannot be serious, Father," he replied.

"Why ever not? You are a more than respectable age for marriage. An alliance between our two kingdoms would be advantageous on both sides. You yourself have said you are not interested in marrying for love. So why not the Sova girl? Is she hideous or something?"

"Of course not," he responded. Skies above, he had found her to be quite the opposite. He should not have used Geri to spy on her in the forest, but he couldn't resist. Watching her sprint through the trees, her thick, dark hair streaming behind her, her face flushed with anger at her brother and his councilors had been quite a sight. She had seemed half wild among the trees. With her God's Gift of speed, she had seemed almost like one of the fae.

"Well then," his father interrupted his thoughts. "It is settled. You will attend the King of Selmy's coronation ball, and you will present yourself as a suitor for the princess. You will make sure she chooses you, and you will return with your betrothed."

"But, Father, I have no interest in settling down with a wife." Especially not a human wife, he added in his head. There was not a drop of fae blood in the Sova line as far as the lineage books had implied. And that was why he could not marry her. He had sworn himself never to fall in love—especially with a human. After watching Marya Sova hold her own in a political meeting of men, and fly through the forest almost as if she had wings herself, he was afraid she would be all too easy to fall in love with.

"Fine, no one will force you to settle down with the girl. Princes and princesses marry for political unions all the time. Marry the girl. Get yourself an heir before I die, so I know our kingdom is safe. Then you can go back to gallivanting across the realm in that ship of yours for all I care, but first, get me an heir."

Ferrand could not fathom why his father was so insistent on getting an heir. The older man seemed in perfect health. There would be many years before Ferrand would take the throne, let alone a son of his. Ferrand's younger brother, Louis, was only seventeen and could easily carry on the line someday if need be.

But arguing with his father was never worth it. Half the time, his father seemed to hate him, and the other time it was as if he could not even bother to care what Ferrand did. Ever since his mother died, King Sebastien Couer Faucon was a bitter and miserable man. How he had convinced another woman, Ferrand's step-mother, Lila, to marry him was beyond comprehension. It was one reason Ferrand spent as much time as he did on his ship. It meant staying away from his father.

"You are dismissed," his father commanded him, standing and gesturing towards the large double doors that led to the hallway.

Ferrand exited. Apparently, he would marry Princess Marya Sova. He supposed it would not hurt him to marry her for a political alliance. He would make sure she understood from the start that that was all that there would be between them. Based on her interactions with her brother's council, she was not keen to marry either. If she knew he would let her do as she pleased, she might agree if only to avoid marrying some other court buffoon.

A FEW WEEKS LATER, Ferrand found himself preparing for his voyage to Selmy Island. He had made one more unsuccessful attempt to convince his father to reconsider. He still could not figure out why the king was desperate for an alliance with the seemingly insignificant island kingdom. Winds above, his step-mother, Lila, was practically giddy with excitement to plan a wedding. She had years before Louis, his half brother, was likely to marry, and with her human life-span, she might not live to see it.

Ferrand did not have much of a relationship with his step-mother or half-brother. He spent so little time at the palace that he had had little interaction with them. Lila seemed nice enough, but he could never imagine why she married his father. One day he had returned to the palace from months at sea, and there she was—no explanation. The next time he returned, he had a baby brother.

When Louis was very young, Ferrand spent more time at home. He knew his father would not be helpful in raising the boy. With Lila being human, he felt obligated to take his brother under his wing—literally. He remained long enough to find out about his brother's fae abilities, including wings like his own, and gave him what help he could in learning to use them. Then he returned to the sea. It always called him back. He knew his ancestors were wind fae, but he sometimes wondered if he had some water fae blood in his distant heritage.

He tried to make it home at least once every few months to check in on his brother. That was how he had ended up roped into spying on the Sova family. His father had caught him just before he had planned to leave again.

Ferrand stalked the length of his ship, checking the rigging for the hundredth time. He knew his crew would have gotten it right, but it gave him something to do to occupy his mind. And he enjoyed working on the boat. He had insisted on taking his own ship, knowing that if he were to settle down and create an heir, it may be his last chance to sail her for a time.

Three ships set out from South Shore to Selmy. Though Ferrand's ship was not the largest—having no need for the huge passenger cabins of the other ships—it was the most beautiful. His ship was his pride and joy, and he had spared no expenses on her. His suite of rooms at the palace contained the bare necessities. His wardrobe was minimal, and he had no expensive hobbies like the noblemen of his father's court. But the Falcon's Kiss might just have been the most spectacular ship in the realm.

Her hull was made of the finest wood, and it gleamed in the sun. The best woodworkers had crafted and adorned her with intricate carvings of falcons. Ferrand had insisted on emerald green sails. He never understood why sails were always white. He had her cabins decorated as finely as the guest rooms at the palace, even though he never used them.

He could have taken passengers with him to Selmy, but he chose not to. He wanted one last trip, just him and his men, without all his father's courtiers around. It seemed the entire court was on their way to the ball. He suspected the other boats were like miniature balls, noblemen and women gathering in their elegant dining rooms and ballrooms.

While the invitations had not blatantly spelled out they were looking for a husband for the princess, everyone knew it to be so. And with half the young noblemen in the kingdom and probably every surrounding kingdom heading to the coronation, it was no wonder the young ladies wanted to go too. It was rare that the kingdoms hosted international affairs of such a grand magnitude. Ferrand suspected there would be many more weddings than just his own to plan in the next few months.

What would his father do if he wasn't able to secure Princess Marya's hand? She had not seemed keen on marrying at all. Why would she choose him? She would choose him because he was a prince, and she was a princess. He was the most appropriate match for her. There was only one other eligible prince on the Torraellium continent. Ferrand didn't know the Prince of Ermaine particularly well, but Prince Gavril was even younger than he was, and had not seemed the sort to be interested in marriage either. When they had hosted him several years back, he had had half the court swooning over him but had shown no signs of interest towards any of them.

Marya would have to choose Ferrand. He was the best option for her—unless King Nasir of Wendyl, was there. Though Ferrand highly doubted he would be. He was an elitist. He was the last remaining full-blooded fae on the continent, maybe in the realm, and he hated the humans he ruled over. Nasir had been a warrior in the fae military. Ferrand did not know the full story, but when the Gates to the fae realm were sealed during the Great Fae War, King Nasir was furious to remain trapped in the human realm. He had gone on a rampage, conquering land, and forcing the former King of Wendyl to surrender his kingdom to his control. Rumor had it, he ruled his people with an iron fist, and they were too afraid of him to complain. Ferrand was definitely Princess Marya's best choice, regardless of who else attended the ball.

Ferrand was not sure if that made him feel better or worse. He didn't even want to marry the girl. If she had dozens of prospective choices, he could pretend he tried his best yet didn't succeed.

With his crew taking care of the sailing, Ferrand made his way inside to get a drink. The ship builders had designed the room as a combination pub and ballroom. He had never used it as a ballroom. He invited no one to sail with him and the crew. Typically, the room was where his off-duty men hung out. He kept the liquor and ale stocked, and so long as the men were reasonable about it, he let them enjoy whatever they pleased. There were also card and gaming tables set up around the edge of the room. There was a stage where musicians could play. He had a few men who played various instruments, and sometimes they would take the stage. He knew the stage was really meant for musicians to play for dancing, but they had never had ladies aboard, so the dancefloor and stage went mostly unused.

Ferrand poured himself a drink and sat on a bar stool. What would it be like to have the princess on board the ship? Would sea life appall her? Ferrand had not wanted her to be uncomfortable. He had brought with him a small staff of servants. He usually wouldn't have bothered with it, but he had hired a better cook for the kitchen, and a few footmen to help with dinners and whatever else. He was planning to eat with his betrothed in the formal dining room—something he almost never did. He preferred to eat with his men overeating alone. He didn't care if he was a prince. Skies, he hoped they wouldn't start fawning over him and acting like he was a prince when Princess Marya was aboard.

"Yer Highness."

Ferrand looked up from his drink to find Jacobe, his first mate, hopping up on a stool with a drink in his hand.

"Jacobe," Ferrand greeted him with a nod of his head.

"All's set. We're on track to dock in Selmy in six or seven days."

"Good."

"So, tell me about her," Jacobe said.

"Who?" Ferrand asked.

"This girl we're traveling across the continent for."

"The princess?" Ferrand asked. "There is not much to tell. My father wants me to marry her. So I guess I will do that."

"You've nev'r cared what yer father wanted before," Jacobe replied. "Ye sure ye don't want to marry the girl?"

"You overstep your boundaries," Ferrand replied. How could he explain to Jacobe why he did or did not want to marry Princess Marya?

"Yer the one who tells us, crew, to pretend yer not a prince when it's just us. You've heard countless stories about our conquests with women. This is the first I've ever known ye to even consider a woman, and yer not going to talk?"

"I am not sure what to say about her, Jac. I do not even know her."

"That's fair, I s'pose," he replied. "So get to know her. When's the last time ye were with a woman?"

"Jacob," Ferrand warned. "I have told you not to treat me as a prince, but I am still your captain, and I do not have to answer that."

"That long, eh?"

"Yes. It's been a while. All right? So what?" Ferrand snapped.

"I mean, I don't know much about ye demi-fae. But as far's I know, yer still a man. That can't be easy."

Ferrand wanted to growl at him. Of course, it wasn't easy! It wasn't like he was a virgin, but he was a Skies-damned prince. Princes couldn't sleep around with random women, and he would not become involved with a human woman. Considering there was only one demi fae woman that he knew of on the entire continent, and she was likely involved with King Nasir, that would not happen.

"Think of it this way," Jacobe continued. "Even if ye don't want to marry the girl, at least ye'll have a warm body in yer bed."

Ferrand felt a rush of blood to his groin at the thought. The princess was undoubtedly attractive. But she was a princess. She shouldn't just be a warm body in someone's bed. When he took her into his bed—for he would have to eventually if his father wanted an heir—would he be able to keep it purely physical? Ferrand had difficulty keeping things purely physical. It was why it had been so long since a woman warmed his sheets. What would it be like with his wife?

FOR THE NEXT FEW DAYS, Ferrand concentrated on sailing his ship, as a distraction. He lost himself in the ocean waves. The weather was calm for the entire trip, and with Ferrand using his fae connection to the air, he kept their sails filled with wind. They arrived at Selmy Island earlier than expected.

As they neared the port city, Ferrand noticed the shape of an enormous bird flying towards them. He was pleased to see Geri. It had seemed silly for her to fly back to Southshore when he would head to Selmy himself.

Ferrand stripped off his shirt, summoning his wings, and leaped into the air to greet her. Geri was his best friend. He had sent her on scouting missions before, but this was the longest they had been apart. He could not remember the time before she had been in his life. No one in the human realm quite understood the bond some fae and demi-fae had with their familiars—or even where it came from. Sometime in Ferrand's childhood, she had appeared one day and began speaking into his mind. They had been inseparable ever since.

Ferrand smiled when he reached her, and she butted her head against him playfully.

Rand, she spoke into his mind. *Missed you, Rand.*

"I missed you too, girlie," he cooed, soaring back down to the deck of the ship.

Geraldine landed next to him on the deck; she reached almost to his waist. He leaned down and scratched her on the head. She nuzzled her head into him, and he wrapped his wing around her protectively. The feathered pattern on their wings was almost identical in varying shades of brown. Geri was the only girl he had ever needed. He wondered how she would feel about sharing him with a wife.

Their bond was powerful enough to communicate over the interminable distance between the two kingdoms. Because it strained both of them, he had only done it a few times. He missed her dearly.

What do you think, Ger? Should I marry the princess?

Like Princess Marya, Geri's voice was warm in his mind. *Princess is nice.*

If Geri liked her, Ferrand knew she was something special. That was the problem. Something special did not make for a strictly political union.

III

Marya

The evening of the coronation came quickly. They had pushed the date back two weeks from the initial plan. They wanted time to invite members of various foreign courts. It still might not have been long enough to expect many of them to attend, but tradition in Selmy did not allow for them to postpone it any longer.

Thank Otreus, the ceremony had gone off without a hitch. Quick. Formal. Boring. And then, suddenly, Marya was making her grand entrance into the ball and wishing she could be anywhere else.

The council, her sister Anna, and their diligent household staff had pulled together a very elegant event on short notice. She thought it seemed inappropriate to have a ball so soon after their parents' death. They were in mourning for Skies' sake.

But here they were.

She looked around the room. Anna and the staff had outdone themselves. That didn't surprise her. Anna had always been her mother's shadow when she planned events. The staff had draped swaths of purple and gold fabric artfully around the room, and candles in glittering crystal holders shimmered along every wall. It all came together with Marya's favorite part of the ballroom, the ceiling. Swirls of deep midnight blue graced the ceiling with shimmering stars speckled across it. Nearly one hundred owls, the Sova family's mascot, hung from the starry mural. They were made from every material imaginable: wooden owls, glass owls, owls molded out of different metals, especially copper. Copper adornments were everywhere. From the wall sconces to the punch bowls, and even the accessories she and her sisters wore. There was no question that copper was in abundance throughout their kingdom.

She continued to survey the room, noting its occupants. This was not their typical ball. A few of their closest friends were in attendance, but instead of the usual courtiers with whom she was familiar, there were many guests from other kingdoms whom she did not recognize. The men outnumbered the women two to one. Though, Marya noted, there were quite a few foreign women in attendance as well. Perhaps they had known about all the men and came to catch husbands themselves.

The foreigners stood out, wearing a much more restrained color pallet. It surprised Marya the differences in fashion on the continent. The cut of their finery was very similar to Selmy Island, with the men wearing fine tailored jackets and slim trousers, while the women wore poufy ball gowns, but their colors were quieter. The men mostly wore black or grey, and the women wore pale pastels or even white. They contrasted heavily with the bright rainbow of colors the Selmy men and women wore. The visitors' jewelry and accessories were mostly made of gold and silver, unlike the copper adorning most of the guests from Selmy.

Marya's own dress was a vivid blue, the color of the ocean on a cloudless day, accented with a copper chain belt that dangled down one side almost to the ground. She hadn't wanted to wear such a bright color, feeling it was too soon to be out of mourning, but her uncle had insisted it was fine. She wore a lacy black shawl, pinned at the neckline of her bodice with one of her mother's copper broaches and a thin chain bearing a copper owl with emerald eyes. She had asked her maid to pin a matching piece of black lace into her hair. The lace draped artfully over her face. She wasn't one for fashion, but she thought she looked quite lovely—though she knew it wasn't her charming face that the men had come for. Her dowry was large, and her title even larger.

Marrying a princess did not automatically make one royalty, but it placed the husband a step above all the other nobility.

And, if it hadn't been obvious why they had made Ivan's coronation into a grand affair, it would be obvious now, with the guest list made up of mostly eligible men. It surprised her to see that no one from Azria on the western continent, Dudaimash was in attendance. The Azrians were their closest neighbors across the sea to the west, and the biggest potential threat, if what the council said was true. Marya knew little about the Azrians, but she knew an alliance with them would be mutually beneficial.

Uncle Tavar had instructed Marya to take every dance offered by nobility from the other kingdoms, and Ivan had agreed. She could not imagine what had gotten into him. He had never cared what she did before, and she'd thought he understood her wishes to stay by his side and rule together. If he hadn't known it before, she made herself plenty clear at the council meeting.

Marya hated being used this way. But she didn't see much of a choice. The council and Ivan would not let her do anything useful if she stayed in Selmy, anyway. Marya had tried to speak to Uncle Tavar again, but he would not hear it. And he refused to inform her of any further council meetings.

Marya was used to court functions, and she didn't hate dancing most of the time. Usually, she danced a few dances with the sons of her father's councilors, and then she and Olga would chat off to the side, joking about the courtiers and how silly they all were. But this time, she would need dance the entire night. Her stomach was in knots, and she itched for a run. Her family, and much of the court, were used to her Gift and her daily runs, but something told her if she left the ball that was being thrown essentially for her, her brother and Uncle Tavar would not be happy. So, she took deep breaths, willing her body to calm down. It helped a bit.

Marya's first dance was with a young count from Wendyl. He was barely old enough to marry and painfully polite. She could not imagine him as a husband. He blushed and stammered and seemed nervous to even touch her. It was clear this was one of the first balls he had attended. He was clearly not the one she would choose. Though she supposed, if she wanted to marry someone she might mold into her ideal husband, he seemed pliable enough. However, that didn't sit well with her. She wanted a husband that saw her as an equal and let her make her own decisions because he respected her opinions, not because he was a doormat.

When the dance was over, she thanked him and had barely a moment to breathe before being pulled into a dance with an older gentleman—perhaps a duke, she couldn't even remember—from Southshore. The dance started off polite enough until she noticed that his gaze never made it to her face, lingering over her body.

"Excuse me, my lord, I cannot help but notice that you seem to have an aversion to my face. Is there something wrong with it? Please be so kind as to let me know so I may make my excuses and recompose myself if need be."

She almost laughed out loud when his eyes snapped to her own. Color stained his cheeks at her chastisement. She wondered if anyone had ever dared to point out his rude behavior before. If he was a duke, most likely not. She was most likely the only woman with a title greater than his own that he had ever shared a dance with.

"Of course not, your highness," he finally replied. "Your face is every bit as lovely as the rest of you."

The audacity! Had he just confirmed that he had been admiring her body?

Marya was only too happy when the dance ended. She walked off without even a "Thank you."

Marya danced with a few more men, so uninteresting she immediately forgot anything about them, before deciding she needed a break.

She looked around the room for her sisters. Surely no one expected her to dance for every moment of the night. She spied Olga standing alone across the room, and she made her way towards her sister. Before she had reached her, however, another gentleman approached her, this one old enough to be her grandfather.

"May I have this dance, your highness?"

Was she expected to consider men like this one? No one had said they would force her to marry the first man to ask, but she did not wish to risk it. If these were the men she would dance with, she would have to make herself as unappealing as possible. Marya preferred to talk with her dance partners, but she held herself back with Lord Grandfather.

No need to make him think she was interested.

"You have a lovely palace here in Selmy," the man commented.

"Thank you," Marya replied.

"I visited once many years ago," he continued.

Skies! How old was this man? Selmy had not hosted foreign dignitaries in her lifetime. She was relatively confident that she had once heard someone say that the reason the Digby family was so prolific was that they were afraid they would run out of suitable marriage pairings for their children. When was the last time they had brought in fresh faces?

"I am sure much has changed since your last visit," Marya replied, hoping her slight at his age appeared accidental.

"I would love a tour of the palace to see some of these changes for myself," he replied. When his hand started a tour from her hips to her bottom, she stifled a gag. Marya shifted her position to move his hand back to its proper place.

"Oh? Will you be staying in Selmy long? I am sure My Uncle Tavar would love to give you a tour on the morrow. He loves sharing our family history." Had that been clear enough that she was uninterested? Foisting him off on her uncle instead of offering to take him herself?

"I am afraid we will only stay the one night," he replied. "Our ship sets sail tomorrow."

"Pity. I am afraid Uncle Tavar is likely too busy enjoying the ball this evening for tours," she replied, hoping he would get the picture.

"Of course," he replied, making no further attempt at conversation.

When the song ended, she noticed Olga had moved. She needed a few moments of peace. Tavar had forbidden her from declining dances, but he had not expressly told her she could not take a break if no one asked her to dance. The balcony doors were nearby. If she could just slip outside for a moment—

Another gentleman caught her elbow before she could make her retreat. Marya debated shaking herself free and exiting the room, but she could not be sure whether her uncle was watching. Was it worth risking the lecture she would receive to avoid another dance with some fool she had no intention of marrying?

"Princess Marya, I presume?" The deep timbre of the masculine voice melted over her like warm honey. The sultry sound had her stopping in her tracks.

Marya turned, expecting to find another old man or pompous aristocrat yearning for a status boost. But she found herself looking into a pair of deep blue eyes almost identical to the color of the ocean and incidentally her dress. Marya's pulse quickened as her eyes roved across his flawless copper-brown skin to the silky black tresses framing his face in long strands that curled at the ends and brushed the collar of his shirt.

"Are you Princess Marya?" he asked again.

Marya swallowed, begging her voice to return to her. She settled for nodding her head. With this effect on her, she would not have to pretend to be vapid and uninteresting, for every sensible thought she had ever possessed seemed to have escaped her head at the sight of the handsome man before her.

"May I have this dance?" he asked.

Marya nodded again, still finding speech beyond her current capabilities.

When the gentleman took her hand in his own, the warmth of his skin broke her trance at last. She noted a roughness to his skin against her ungloved fingers that was uncommon in the hands of the nobleman in her acquaintance. Her senses finally returning, she followed him into the dance.

Marya studied the man more closely, avoiding locking eyes with him lest she lose her senses again. He wore a golden circlet on his head that might have looked feminine on most men but seemed appropriate for him and in no way detracted from his masculinity. The muscular frame she felt beneath his jacket set him apart from the foppish men of her court. Who was this man?

Where the other gentleman with whom she had danced had seemed eager to catch her attention, this one seemed set on ignoring her. His dancing skills were impeccable, and he moved with a smooth elegance she had not witnessed in any of her other partners. But he said nothing. He barely even looked at her. If he had not wanted to dance with her, why had stopped her from making her retreat?

When the dance ended, he bowed formally to her and walked away, with no more than a polite "thank you." Marya stared after him, wondering what she had done to offend the gentleman.

Marya was about to make her exit at last when Anna appeared at her side.

"Oh, Marya," she breathed. "Isn't Prince Faucon dreamy?"

"Huh?" Marya asked, barely hearing her sister.

"Prince Ferrand Faucon. From Southshore. I cannot believe you danced with him."

So that was who he was. No wonder he was so graceful. Prince Ferrand Faucon was one of the last fae descendants in the realm. The fae were known for their elegance. No wonder he had been uninterested in her. What would he want with a human princess? It surprised her he had even come.

"You should dance with him again," Anna squealed.

"What for?" Olga asked.

"You looked like a painting," she gushed. "Both of you with your dark hair. And did you notice his smooth skin is almost the exact shade as your copper jewelry?"

"Mmm hmm," Marya replied distractedly. "And his eyes matched my dress, so what?"

"You gazed into his eyes?" Anna was practically jumping. "Marya, you must dance with him again. Here. Let me take this veil off so he can see you properly." Anna reached up and began pulling pins out of Marya's hair and veil. "Your eyes are your best feature. You shouldn't hide them. Oh! Wouldn't it be perfect if he was the one you married?"

Marya was unsure what to say. She should have stopped her sister from removing the lace. However, Anna had surprised her, and she did want to get a better look at Prince Ferrand without the gauzy black material in her way.

"Why would he want to marry me?" Marya asked.

"Why wouldn't he?" Anna squealed. "Marya, I have never seen you like this. You are usually the most confident person I know. You marched into a council meeting and asked them to put you in charge of the kingdom instead of Ivan. He would want to marry you."

Skies. Anna was right. She was acting like the simpering court fools she hated. She hoped he did ask her for another dance so she could show him she was as unaffected by him as he was by her.

But first, she would finally step outside for some air.

Marya stepped out onto the balcony, hoping she could have a moment alone. She looked out over the moonlit courtyard below. A familiar itch crept over her, beginning in her toes and inching up her calves. Marya wanted to run. She couldn't, but she wanted to. Instead, she placed her palms together over her heart. She took in a deep breath, counting to four. She held her breath for another count of four and breathed out for four. She repeated the breathing pattern a few times, willing calm to return to her body. It worked. The breathing and stretching exercises her governess had taught her as a child worked as a temporary solution to her itch. They came in handy when she wanted to run but could not.

Marya returned to the ballroom, and her eyes immediately fell upon the prince. Marya picked her way across the dancefloor to where he stood, talking with another gentleman. If she could demand a room full of old men to consider making her their ruler, she could ask a man to dance instead of waiting around for him. She needed to prove she could remain in control of her wits when he took her into his arms again.

IV

Ferrand

Ferrand stood near to the spot where he had danced with the princess. It had been an effort of will to remain indifferent when he swept her into his arms. He chatted amicably with a young lord from his kingdom, but his mind was on Princess Marya and how he would present himself as the best marriage prospect.

He had barely said a word to her during their dance. She had practically melted into his arms, and her physical attraction to him had radiated off her in waves. Ferrand thanked the Skies she was wearing a mourning veil because he was unsure if he could handle the desire he knew was burning in her eyes.

"Prince Ferrand, I presume?" a melodic voice interrupted his thoughts.

Ferrand looked up to find himself confronted with those very eyes. They were not, however, filled with desire, but an endearing hint of worry. She had removed the black veil. It was the first time Ferrand had seen her up close without it. Her gaze stunned him in place, and he found himself unable to speak. Her emerald eyes glistened in the bright light of the ballroom, and Ferrand could not look away.

Princess Marya's hair had been pulled back from her face, revealing pale creamy skin. He could not help that his eyes followed the curve of her cheek and down the column of her neck. It was a relief to see she had not removed the shawl she had pinned closed with a copper broach. It covered the neckline of her dress, making it easier to bring his gaze back to her face. He imagined what he would find if he unpinned the black lace. The familiar warmth of desire pulsed in his core, and it startled him when she spoke again.

"Prince Ferrand, may I have this dance?" she asked.

No one had ever asked him to dance before. His heartbeat sped up, and a nervous laugh burst from his throat. She stared at him, worrying her bottom lip with her teeth. Was she nervous? Had she really just asked him to dance? A broad grin spread across his face. She was full of surprises.

At his smile, she seemed to relax, smiling back at him and nodding towards the dance floor. Ferrand took her hand in his and led her to an open space near the edge of the crowd. He had remained casual during their first dance, barely speaking or even looking at her. This time, he couldn't help looking down at her with appreciation.

Her brilliant, ocean-blue gown set off the rest of her coloring perfectly. Her long hair was almost as dark as his own, and while it had been partially pulled back from her face, the bulk of it hung down her back in a long smooth sheet. The soft silky strands tickled him, brushing the hand that rested on her waist.

"You know," he said at last. "I have never been asked to dance before."

"I would imagine not," she replied. What did that mean? Was she regretting asking him?

"Is that what it feels like every time a gentleman asks you to dance?" Ferrand asked.

"Like what?" she asked.

"Like time stands still, and you forget where you should look or how to respond."

Her dance step faltered, and he heard her breathing hitch. Princess Marya looked up at him, gazing directly into his eyes, and froze. Skies above! She was gorgeous.

"Not every time, no," she breathed.

"I see." He smiled. Had she felt the same way when he asked her to dance? His stomach fluttered. Skies, it wasn't his first time dancing with an attractive young woman. What was happening to him?

"So, tell me about yourself, Princess Marya," he asked, needing to change the subject to something platonic.

"I am sure there isn't much to tell that you don't already know," she replied. "You must have done your research before you came." She fluttered her lashes at him. She needed to stop looking at him like that.

"I am not sure I understand what you mean," he replied.

"Why surely it comes as no surprise why my brother invited you here. Of course, you know that you are a prospective candidate for my hand in marriage?"

Ferrand wasn't sure how to respond. That was why he was there, but it felt like a trick question.

"I would think anyone who was planning to get into such a contract," she continued, "would do their research before negotiations began."

"Is that what you would consider a marriage? Contract negotiations?" Maybe it would be easier than he thought to keep her at a distance. She clearly was only marrying out of duty.

"Well, not all marriages are like that," she continued. "But surely it would not shock you to find that when the eldest princess of a tiny kingdom is looking to marry outside of her kingdom, that there would be contract negotiations that went along with it. You cannot possibly expect that my brother is hoping I find my true love tonight."

No, he knew that the human nobility rarely married for love. But to hear her say it so casually as if she was unaffected by their dance and the thought of marrying him when he was trembling inside at the effort it took to restrain himself from pulling her closer and letting himself get lost in her. He would need to get ahold of himself.

"I see," he replied, matching her even tone. "As you seem the practical sort, have you deduced from the candidates who would make the most beneficial match to your kingdom?"

He held his breath. He knew that he was the obvious choice as far as political connections went, but would she agree?

"Well, unfortunately for me, as most men do not see women as fit for discussing things such as business agreements and contracts, I fear I will not have much say in the matter," she replied, evading his question. "Most likely, what will happen is that half the men here will seek my brother out tomorrow, all promising the things they will do for Selmy's benefit if only he would grant them my hand in marriage."

"Well, that seems terribly unromantic," he replied.

He thought he felt her breath catch, but she replied calmly. "Oh, I am not looking for romance." If that was true, why had she begun absentmindedly winding her fingers in the loose curls where his hair brushed his shoulders.

"Then what are you looking for?" he asked. His voice came out huskier than he intended, and her pupils dilated slightly at the sound. Ferrand smiled a slow half-smile.

He almost chuckled when she shook herself, blinking to clear the haze from her eyes.

"Well, for starters," her voice was high and breathy, "if I am to be entering contract negotiations, I would like to be the one at the table doing the negotiating." Her words were logical and detached, but her body language was not—she bit her lip again, and he could feel her heart racing. Ferrand couldn't stop looking at her mouth. He wondered what it would feel like pressed against his own, his own teeth lightly nibbling on the soft flesh. He swallowed hard.

"That seems only fair," he replied. He chuckled, imagining her arguing negotiations with his father about what their marriage would mean.

Her usually graceful dancing faltered again. The music was ending anyway. He did not want to let someone else take her away. So before some other gentleman could ask her for a dance, Ferrand led her to a pair of tufted chairs against the wall.

She sat, but it appeared the end of the dance had broken the spell between them. Her gaze flitted around, and she avoided looking directly at his face. Ferrand needed to get her talking again.

"Alright, Princess, if your brother and his council were to take your opinions into consideration, who would you say would make the best political match for your kingdom?" he asked. He wasn't sure why he wanted so badly for her to say aloud that she would choose him.

"I would think it should be quite apparent what would be the best political deal for Selmy," she replied.

"Oh?" he asked.

"Why, that would be Lord Ambrose from Wendyl, of course," she said, smirking at him.

Ferrand chuckled. He did not know who Lord Ambrose was, but if it was any of the men she had danced with before him, they were all absurd choices. "Ah yes, and which one would he be?" he asked. "The young fellow that blushed and stammered every time he looked at you? Or was it the man with the roving eyes that you chastised for his lecherous ways? Or could it be the older gentleman who I had assumed must be an elderly relative of yours?"

Marya stiffened in her chair. Had he offended her? She jiggled her leg anxiously. She looked around the room.

"Are you all right?" he asked.

She swallowed, refusing to meet his eye, her leg continuing to bounce.

"What is it?" he asked. The last time he had seen the panic-stricken look on her face was when he had been watching her through Geri's eyes. She had shown the same expression right before she fled from her brother's council room and tore through the forest. Was she looking for an escape? Maybe she wanted to run like she had.

He would like to see it in person.

"Do you think anyone would notice if we disappeared for a bit?" He asked.

"Excuse me?!" Marya responded, and he realized how he must have sounded.

"I just thought you seem a little tense. I thought you might like to go for a run?"

"A run?" She asked, her voice faint.

"Yes. A run. Maybe in the forest?"

"I'm not sure what you're talking about." She had stopped her frantic wiggling, looking like a rabbit who'd just caught sight of its predator. Was she frightened of him? Of course, she was! He had just admitted that he been spying on her during a private moment.

"I'm sorry. It's just- you have Otreus's Gift, don't you?" he asked.

"How do you know that?" she asked.

"Oh, a little birdie told me. Well, actually a rather big birdie." he chuckled slightly at his joke.

He knew the moment realization dawned on her; her eyes going wide with surprise.

"The falcon?" She stiffened again. "Were you spying on our family? What were you doing here?"

"Well, actually, I wasn't here at all. Geraldine—that is my familiar—was here. I was at home in Southshore."

"But how did you- can you see through her eyes?" A spark of curiosity lit her eyes.

"Yes," he replied. "It is rather taxing on me, but yes." Fascination and annoyance warred in her expression.

"But why were you spying on me?" she asked.

"I wasn't spying on you, exactly," he replied.

"Right, it was your bird," she replied dryly.

"Well, yes, but that's not what I meant. She was not there to spy on you, specifically." He should be honest with her about why his father had sent Geri to spy on them. He wanted to see how her brother was handling the transition to king.

"Listen," Ferrand continued, "if you are to enter into any sort of contract with me, I would want you to know all the facts before you signed anything-"

"Who said I was planning to enter a contract with you?" she interrupted him. Had he messed up his chance? He hadn't originally wanted to marry her, but now he couldn't stand the thought she might say no. He tried to tell himself it was only because of how unbearable his father would be if she refused him. He had to salvage the situation somehow.

"Enough with the game. We both know I am the best prospect you have here. As a prince, I have the highest title here; my kingdom is wealthy and needs little from yours." She seemed to relax again at his appeal to her business mind.

"I will admit I have not conducted many contract negotiations, but I have the general understanding that they usually involve a mutually satisfying outcome for both parties," she replied, transforming into a confident businesswoman. "You said yourself that your kingdom needs nothing from mine. What does Southshore get out of a marriage agreement between you and me?"

I get you, Ferrand wanted to answer. The more time he spent with Princess Marya, the harder, he realized, it would be to keep her at a distance. He was not interested in anything more than friendship with her, however. He had no plans to settle down into married life.

And the princess did not seem interested in romance. As she had said, their arrangement would be a business contract. So, what did Southshore gain from this alliance? It was a question he had been asking himself since his father had first insisted upon it. What was so special about Selmy Island?

"I will be perfectly honest with you, Princess Marya, since you seem to have a head for business," Ferrand replied. "I do not really see the appeal of your kingdom as an ally. I will admit, I have spent more time traveling than learning about my kingdom's foreign affairs, so there may be an angle I am missing. But my father is a greedy man. It may simply be that he wants this alliance so that no one else can have it."

"It seems rather foolish of your father to send you to make a contract negotiation without understanding the terms," she replied. Her face was a cool mask, displaying none of her emotions. He had mostly just insulted her kingdom. Where was the spark he had seen from her previously?

"It is possible that my father only wanted the prestige of winning the alliance, and terms don't matter to him."

"Well, Prince Ferrand," she said. "We both know that you are my best option, aside from what is in it for Selmy, what is in it for me? My brother made it clear he will not force me to marry anyone if I have strong reservations against it. So, tell me. Why should I choose you?"

Ferrand swallowed. With all her talk of contracts and politics, he was unprepared for her question. What could he offer her that no one else here could?

"I must admit. I don't rightly know," he replied. "You said yourself you were not interested in marriage. I could offer you the usual promises and romance that most men would offer, but something tells me that is not what you want. You tell me. What can I give you?"

Ferrand held his breath, waiting for her reply. If he had misjudged her and she was looking for more than just a platonic business deal, would he be able to turn her down? Would he want to?

Princess Marya looked into his eyes. She was assessing him. Ferrand felt a jolt of heat, hoping that she liked what she saw. With a heightened sense of smell from his Fae bloodline, he had scented her reaction to him during their first encounter. He knew she was attracted to him physically, but he had a sudden desire to know what she thought of him as a person.

"Well, how can we make this mutually beneficial to both of us?"

"What do you mean?"

"What is it that you do want?"

She stared at him. She was clearly taken aback. Had no one ever asked her before what she wanted?

"Freedom." She suggested tentatively.

"Freedom?" He questioned.

"Freedom to be myself. To have more to do than attend parties and balls. To have my opinions valued. For my husband to treat me as an equal."

"Oh, is that all?" He asked.

"Is that all? I should think it is enough. Are you honestly prepared to offer it?"

"I think I can arrange it. Though with the long lifespans of my family, it may take some time before I have a say in the ruling of my kingdom."

"But why?" She asked suspiciously. "Why do you want to marry a woman you just met? About whom you know hardly anything? A woman that you know is only in it for the political advantages?"

"What woman isn't in it for the political advantages when marrying a prince? Besides, I may not know how yet, but it is advantageous for my kingdom. Or I assume my father will make it so."

"And I could really be your equal?" she asked

"I must say, I have had little involvement in the politics of running my kingdom thus far. If you marry me, I will not only let you assist me, but I will most likely rely on you as you probably know more about running a kingdom than I do."

She chuckled. The laugh bubbled out of her like a babbling brook. Ferrand tried to think of something clever he could say to hear a repeat.

"Why is it you know so little about running your kingdom?" she asked.

"As you might have guessed, my father is not my favorite person. I spend as little time in his presence as possible. I spend most of my time on my sailing ship. I also enjoy freedom, you might say."

"I suppose you are one of the more tolerable men here. You really think an agreement between us would suit you?"

Here was his out. She was letting him say no. He could walk away and pretend someone else had claimed her. But then she would be stuck marrying some other noble who wouldn't give her the chance to be herself. She would make a damned fine queen someday.

"Prince Ferrand, you hesitate. Are you sure it's what you want? I am in no short supply of suitors. I will not force you."

"Yes," he blurted before he could stop himself.

"Fine." She said. "It's a deal." She put out her hand as if to shake on a business contract. Her voice was flat, almost bored, but he hoped the twinkle in her eyes meant that she was pleased with the match.

He took her hand as if to shake, but instead, he pulled it to his lips, placing a single feather-light kiss on the back of her knuckles.

"It's a deal," he agreed.

LATER THAT NIGHT, FERRAND lay awake, unable to sleep, in the cabin of his ship, wondering if he had made the right choice. Skies above, he could not stop thinking about her.

After they shook on their arrangement, Ferrand had asked her for another dance. Three dances in one night would let any other potential suitors know he had staked his claim. When they returned to the floor, her Uncle's eyes had landed on them. His satisfied smile was enough to let Ferrand know the match pleased him.

With their agreement settled, he had found his heart racing as they danced. He pulled her closer than he probably ought to have, and he felt her heart beating in time with his own. Three dances and his body was on fire for her. How would he keep her at a distance? She was everything he could have wanted in a wife. She was intelligent, strong, and possibly the most beautiful woman he had ever laid eyes on.

She was perfect in nearly every way—except that she was one hundred percent full-blooded human.

42

V

Marya

The next morning Marya awoke with the feeling that storm clouds were hovering above her. Had she really agreed to marry a fae prince? It had seemed like the right choice the previous night, but she did not feel as sure in the light of day. She had to choose someone. She was starting to see that it was the only way she, as a woman, could help the kingdom. At least, Prince Ferrand would be more interesting than most of the noblemen she had met in her life.

She still knew nothing about him, however. He had agreed to help his father spy on her family. Was his father so desperate to prove his kingdom was the best that he would send his son to solidify a marriage alliance his kingdom didn't even need? That did not sit well with her. No one negotiated a contract without making sure there was something in it for them—not even a marriage contract. She would need to be vigilant around King Faucon. Maybe she could figure out his angle before he and Ivan negotiated their agreement.

Marya had expected to have more time at home with her family. But Prince Ferrand was eager to set sail. And it seemed their guests all wished to depart quickly. Everything around her was a flurry of activity.

It was hard for Marya to stay in her self-inflicted sour mood when all around her everyone buzzed with excitement. Her maid, Ellie, had woken her before the sun so they could ready her belongings. Marya could not stop yawning. She had barely slept a few hours between the late end to the ball and her early morning.

She begged Ellie to pack her simplest gowns, including her corset free dresses, for traveling. They would be on a boat, and it was not as if there would be anyone to impress. She would ride on Prince Ferrand's personal vessel, and apparently, none of the other guests had traveled with him. Ellie had insisted she would want to look her best for her future husband. Marya didn't understand why. The arrangements were already made. It was not like he would back out, in the middle of the ocean, just because she didn't wear her loveliest gown. Eventually, they compromised that Ellie would pack more formal dresses for dinner, and she would let Marya dress more casually during the day.

After hours of preparations, Marya sat on the sofa in her sitting room, nervously tapping her foot as she watched an endless parade of footmen taking trunks and packages out to the carriages that were waiting to bring them to the harbor.

A knock sounded on the door.

"Come in," Marya called.

Olga and Anna entered. Anna threw herself down on the sofa next to Marya. "I cannot believe you are leaving us to marry a faerie prince," she squealed.

"One-quarter fae," Olga corrected, sitting primly on a nearby armchair.

"You've studied his lineage?" Marya asked. "Maybe you want to marry him instead of me?"

"For all that you followed Father around learning how to run the kingdom, you never learned about the important members of the other kingdoms?" Olga asked.

"Of course, I knew of the Faucon family, and even that they were descended from wind fae, but, no, I had not memorized their family tree."

"I knew he would want to marry you once you danced with him again, Marya," Anna said.

Marya rolled her eyes. "It is a political alliance and nothing more. His father sent him with the express intention of marrying me." And she was going to find out why.

"He could have let someone else have you," Anna argued. "He chose you. You should have seen the way he looked at you, Mar. He was watching you like a hawk all evening."

"Like a falcon," Olga laughed.

"Enough, you two," Marya begged them.

"Olga, you better find a husband soon too. I want my turn," Anna giggled. "You should have been looking last night, too. We could have taken out two birds with one stone."

"I hardly think a ball is where I will find a husband. You have seen me dance. Besides, every man there had his attention on Marya. I will just tell Uncle Tavar and Ivan to choose someone for me and be done with it."

Anna rolled her eyes.

When Ivan came to tell her that her carriage was ready, Marya felt a prickle of tears in her eyes. Selmy Castle was her home. She did not want to leave. Her siblings walked with her down to the front steps of the palace. Anna sobbed into her shoulder when Marya enveloped her in a hug. Even Olga sniffled when they said their goodbyes.

Ivan stood awkwardly, shifting his weight between his feet. He seemed unsure if he should hug her or not. Marya took pity on him and hugged him as well. "Mother would be happy," Ivan murmured. That was all he had to say to her about sending her off to another kingdom to marry a stranger?

"Don't make it a long engagement," Anna called to her, as Marya stepped into the carriage that would take her to meet her future husband. "We want to visit sooner rather than later."

WHEN THEY ARRIVED AT the harbor, it felt almost like another party. Servants bustled about helping the visitors prepare for their departures. Everyone agreed it would not be polite to overstay their welcome while the family was grieving.

Of course, Marya hadn't been given a proper chance to grieve, before being swept away to another kingdom, to make plans immediately for a wedding—to a man she hardly knew.

With so many leaving all at once, everyone in the city had gathered to see off the foreigners. Southshore had been the only kingdom to send their prince. But at least thirty other wealthy families were departing, with hundreds of servants milling about. Marya noted a few of her servants in their purple livery loading her belongings onto the smallest, yet most extravagant of the ships.

Marya's pulse quickened at the thought of spending approximately a week on the small ship, alone with the prince. Well, not alone. There would be servants and the rest of the ship's crew. But she would know no one except for her maid and her future husband—a man whom she knew almost nothing about.

She thought back to their dances the previous night, remembering the feel of his calloused hands holding her own and his deep, blue eyes that had felt as if they could see into her soul. Maybe they could. She knew little about fae magic. He might have an ability, like Anna's, to read her thoughts. Marya shivered, imagining him seeing her personal thoughts about him—the way her body had reacted to his deep voice, and his firm touch.

The harbor was a cacophony as Marya made her way to Prince Ferrand's ship. In addition to the passengers and their servants, merchants shouted at the crowd, hoping to make a few last sales before they boarded their ships.

It was rare to have so many passengers and ships in the harbor at once. Usually, there were only dockworkers, merchants, and their crewmen. Marya had heard the nobility on the mainland often visited each other, but as far back as Marya could remember, no one of note had ever come to Selmy Island.

As she drew near, Marya gaped at the six large ships waiting to take the noble families and their servants back to their kingdoms. Up close, she realized Prince Ferrand's small vessel was still quite large. Three ships had come from Southshore, but Marya was to ride the prince's ship. Falcon's Kiss, it was named. How fitting.

She thought about the brush of his lips on her fingers and wondered how they would feel in a proper kiss. The journey would take them five or six days, almost a week. Would she find out before they reached Southshore?

Marya shook her head to clear it. She would focus on the trip itself. Considering she had been raised on an island, it was strange that she had never been on a voyage by sea before. She and her siblings were sheltered. They had never been off the island. Father had promised to take them on a trip someday, but it had never happened. And now it never would.

Marya's insides were in knots as she tried to untangle her messy thoughts. Excitement about sailing, anxiety about her future husband, the pang of sadness at leaving her family. What if she ended up hating Prince Ferrand? He had seemed genuine when he promised to treat her as his equal and to take her on adventures, but what if there was something else in it for him, she hadn't considered?

They loaded up the boat, and Marya stood by the rail, watching the shores of Selmy slip away from them. The sun was sinking lower and lower on the horizon, streaks of gold and pink slashed across the sky, fading to deep shades of violet and blue. Marya watched the moon come into view, a shining crescent in the sky that evening. It had been a similar crescent on the night her parents had returned from a voyage to the Southern continent of Ozoth, bringing with them the sickness that led to their death. The moon had cycled five, maybe six times since then—she had lost count.

She watched the moonrise, and the sunset, wishing to go back in time and spend more of it with her parents, especially her mother. She had spent so much time learning the kingdom with her father; she had not given her mother enough time. She knew her mother loved her, but she wished they had expressed their affections to one another more frequently.

She was not ready to deal with those thoughts. Getting upset made her itch for a run, which she had a feeling would not be possible for a while. So, she pushed herself away from the rail and searched for her husband-to-be.

Marya found Prince Ferrand on an upper deck. Had she not looked closely, Marya might have assumed he was one of the crew. He wore the same fitted leather pants as the sailors, and he had stripped off his shirt. She had not realized in his court finery how muscular he was. Her heart thumped hard in her chest as she watched him. She noticed subtle differences in his mannerisms that set him apart from the other men. He seemed more elegant. His movement was purposeful and fluid, like silk.

Men scurried around him, moving things around and tying ropes to other things. She really would have to learn ship terminology if she were to travel with him in the future. Marya refused to be an ornament on his ship. She would learn to pull her weight.

She felt the moment Prince Ferrand noticed her watching him. He had been ordering the men about, and as he gestured towards the lower deck where she stood, she saw his entire demeanor change when his eyes alighted on her. His silken grace became stiffer, and he forced a smile onto his face. Marya bit her lip and averted her gaze, hoping he hadn't seen the disappointment on her face.

Was the thought of marrying her that unpleasant for him? He had seemed willing the previous night. Or had he? She remembered his hesitation. Was he regretting his decision? Marya fought to contain the worry rushing over her. She had known they agreed to a marriage of convenience and nothing more. She had offered him the chance to change his mind, and he had not taken it.

Despite his awkwardness, after giving a few more commands to the crew, the prince descended a set of stairs, heading straight towards her.

"Good afternoon, Princess," he greeted her, his smile broadening to something more believable.

"Prince," she responded. She could not help the way her gaze drifted over his chiseled arms and broad chest. His answering smirk showed her he was completely aware of where her attention was. Her cheeks colored.

"What do you think of the Falcon's Kiss?" he asked, emphasizing the name of his ship. His smirk did not falter, and the glint in his eyes implied the double meaning was intentional.

"I have little to compare it to," she said, attempting to hold her voice steady. And it was true on all accounts. Her kissing experience was as lacking as her experience with sea travel. "Perhaps you could teach me a thing or two."

Her reply startled the prince; his gaze immediately strayed towards her lips. She bit her lower lip, a nervous habit she would have to break if it would always cause his eyes to flare like that. Her heart beat faster and harder. It would be a surprise if the prince could not hear its erratic rhythm.

"Come, I will give you a tour," he responded, dropping the dangerous game they were playing and offering her his arm.

Marya placed her hand on his bare arm, trying to pretend it was natural. If he could step away from the flirting so easily, surely, she could learn to as well. But her heart continued to hammer in her chest, and she could not ignore the firm muscles under her fingers.

Marya tried to pay attention to the prince's tour as best as she could. He took her to an inner deck. She cursed herself for immediately forgetting what he had called it. She found herself impressed. Even though they were aboard a ship and things were smaller, they were no less opulent than she would have expected from one of the manor homes of the courtiers she knew. There were six passenger cabins, though all remained empty, except for hers and his.

Prince Ferrand showed her to her cabin first. Her maid, Ellie, had already found her way there and was unpacking Marya's belongings into a finely carved oak wardrobe built right into the wall of the cabin.

"You don't have to do that, Ellie. We will be on board for less than a week. I can live out of a trunk."

"Of course, I will be unpacking for you, my lady," Ellie replied. "I can't have you wearing rumpled dresses to dinner, now, can I? Besides, what else am I to do to keep busy but take care of you?"

Marya had known Ellie would insist, but it never hurt to try.

Prince Ferrand remained in the hallway outside her room while she and Ellie chatted. Marya tried not to look at him. The idea of that hulking, bare-chested man just outside her bedroom door had her feeling hot all over. Would she ever get used to his presence, even when they were married? Prince Ferrand seemed determine to skirt the boundaries of propriety just close enough to send her heart racing, but without overstepping. It was maddening.

After showing a quick peek at a few of the empty bunks, they made their way to the dining room. Thank Oola, they had not looked in on the prince's room. Though he had pointed out the door as they walked by. He also told her about the bunks for the crew forbidding her to visit them. Did he really think she was crazy enough to visit the rooms of two dozen strange men?

The dining room was tiny, but every bit as elegant as the one in her own palace. Well, her brother's palace. She supposed it was no longer her home. She stopped in the middle of the dining room, frozen by the sobering thought that she had left her home—possibly for the last time.

"Is everything alright, Princess?"

"Yes. No. I don't know. It's- It's just-" Her voice came out high and shaky.

"Come," the prince commanded, taking her hand and leading her out of the dining room. He brought her to another inner room. It looked like it could serve many purposes. One half of the room appeared to be for dancing. A magnificent chandelier hung over a small dance floor, and there was a small, raised platform big enough for a few musicians. Maybe a quartet at most. It was like a miniature version of the ballrooms she was used to.

Across the dance floor were several tables and chairs. Each table had a unique gaming pattern painted on it. There was a built-in compartment for marbles, cards, and other game pieces. Past the tables, which was where the prince led her, was a bar. It looked almost like a small version of a bar in a tavern. It had room for a few people to sit, and behind it was a large cabinet filled with assorted bottles of what Marya assumed was liquor.

The prince gestured to one of the bar stools. Marya was glad she had chosen a dress with a slim skirt. She had never climbed up on a barstool before, and she could imagine one of her larger dresses would have made the task more difficult. Prince Ferrand made his way around to the other side of the bar. Marya gave a wry chuckle at the idea of a prince serving as a bartender.

"What will it be, m'lady," he asked, imitating the speech of a working-class man.

"Funny. I'm sure you could have guessed that I have spent little time in taverns. Do you have a winterberry wine by chance? Considering they are pretty much the only fruit that grows in abundance in my kingdom, I'm afraid that's all I'm used to drinking."

"Unfortunately, I do not. Though I have a feeling our trade negotiations with Selmy will improve significantly over the coming months." he winked at her.

Marya wasn't sure whether to be offended or flattered. No one had ever winked at her before. Despite her unhappiness, she felt a delicious squirm in her belly.

"Well then, pour me whatever the young ladies in your court drink. I'm sure it will do."

"Well, this might surprise you to know, I have minimal experience tending bar for the young ladies in my court. I can tell you what the crew likes to drink on my ship, and what the male courtiers prefer when they gamble and game, but I haven't the faintest idea what the young ladies prefer."

"Alright, I'll have whatever you're having."

The prince grabbed two short glasses from the shelf behind him, and a bottle of deep orange liquid. He poured them each a glass and passed one across the table.

"I've heard tell, from my men of course, that a bartender is an excellent person with whom to unburden one's sorrows," he said dramatically.

"Is that so?" She asked. "And am I to assume that you are acting the role of the listening bartender?" Marya asked.

"Why not?"

"You could probably guess at what is going through my head, seeing as how you are all tangled up in the mess of it." She took a sip of the orange liquor. It was sweet and a bit spicy. It was not a drink she would have pictured the prince enjoying. Her heart jumped at the thought that he had probably chosen it, not because he liked it, but because he hoped she would. His constant change in demeanor was confusing her. He said he wanted nothing more than a political marriage, but he was being so kind to her. And though she had little experience, she was sure she had seen desire in his eyes when he looked at her. Did he enjoy the same rush of heat she felt when she looked at him?

VI

Ferrand

Ferrand's heart plummeted into his stomach, knowing that he caused Princess Mayra's morose mood. But it should not have surprised him. She had been just as reluctant to marry as he had. Was she having second thoughts?

"Pretend that I am some stranger in a tavern and tell me your troubles," he said. He could not let her sit there in sadness. No matter how much he tried to keep her at a distance, he found himself pulling her closer.

"I am sure you can guess. I lost my parents. My kingdom is a mess. I've left my home, my brother, and my sisters. And- and I never wanted to get married. But here we are. I am betrothed, and my intended is practically a stranger." Her voice cracked on her last sentence, and he could tell she was doing everything she could to hold back her tears.

Ferrand made his way back to her side of the bar and hopped onto the stool next to her. He reached his hand out and covered her own where it rested on the bar top. She flinched when their hands made contact, but she seemed to relax after a moment. Ferrand wondered if the same warm tingle that overcame him had surprised her as well.

"Well, I cannot do anything to bring your parents back. I know how deeply that hurts. I lost my mother many years ago, and I still miss her every day. And as for your kingdom, that is the primary reason we are getting married, right? It will be good for both of our kingdoms. We will figure out what to do to help your brother's kingdom." Ferrand absently rubbed his thumb on the back of her delicate hand. It reminded him of the seductive kisses he had placed there the previous evening.

Marya sniffed and took another sip of her drink with her free hand. It pleased him that she did not pull away her other hand, so he continued to stroke it. He was doing some job keeping his distance from the entrancing young human beside him.

"And as for your intended being a stranger," he murmured, his voice low and sensual despite himself. "He would like for you to get to know him better, Princess."

She looked up from her drink; her green eyes shimmered with unshed tears. Ferrand's breath caught in his throat at the raw and beautiful emotion he saw there. Without thinking, he turned his body towards her. Reaching up, he placed his free hand on her cheek. As if it had been waiting for someone who might brush it away, a single tear made its way down her creamy skin. Ferrand brushed it away with his thumb. Princess Marya closed her eyes, leaning into the touch.

His heart hammered in his chest. Ferrand longed to pull her into his arms and soothe her. But he knew it would not be right. He should not lead her on that way if he planned to keep his distance—and he was still planning to keep her at a distance, wasn't he?—It would be a cruel thing to make her love him when he knew he couldn't love her in return. No, Ferrand would start putting up boundaries.

Removing his hand from her face, and bringing their joined hands to his mouth, he gave her a quick kiss on the back of her hand. He restrained himself, keeping it chaste, when what he wanted was to kiss each knuckle before trailing his mouth to her wrist, and down her arm-

Ferrand dropped her hand quickly before he did something he would regret.

"I must attend to my crew now," he said. It was a poor excuse, but he had to get away from her before he threw caution to the wind and kissed her senseless.

"Make yourself at home."

Princess Marya opened her eyes, looking at him in surprise, which quickly turned to hurt. He hated himself for adding to her troubles, but

it was better this way. He gave her a curt nod and fled the room. Her gaze burned into him. "Dinner is served in an hour," he called behind him without even a backward glance.

SITTING AT THE LONG wooden table in the ship's main dining room, Ferrand felt nervous in a way he could not remember feeling in all his long years. He was anxious about dining with his betrothed. He craved nothing more than to woo her into his arms, but he would remain casual and distanced. His head spun, thinking about it.

Princess Marya entered the dining room in a lovely evening gown. In his kingdom, women typically dressed in flowier cooler garments for the heat, but he knew that was not the case in Selmy or the other kingdoms around him. Even the women from Southshore had donned poofy ballgowns at the Selmy ball. He preferred this sleeker evening gown Marya wore for dinner to the ridiculous, frothy ballgowns—though Marya had looked stunning in her ball gown too.

Her dinner dress was emerald, almost identical to the color of her eyes, and cut slim through her torso, accentuating every curve of her figure until it flared out in a small bell at her hips. She wore a black lace shawl like the one she had worn at the ball, or possibly the same one. The human custom of wearing black in honor of a deceased loved-one fascinated him. The fae and demi-fae mourned their loved ones, but instead of honoring them with sadness, they celebrated them, and then life moved on. This was one fae custom his father kept, though Ferrand didn't know where his father learned of it, having also grown up in the human realm.

Ferrand stood, nodding politely. He had instructed the footmen to set her a place at the opposite end of the long table from his. They remained unmarried, after all, and he knew the human custom in Southshore involved moving the wife's place next to her husband on the evening of the wedding. He could only assume it was the same in Selmy. It suited Ferrand better for keeping her at a distance, anyway.

Princess Marya did not seem surprised by the arrangement, but he noticed her eyes flicked for the briefest of moments towards the chair at his side. In time, she would sit there. But there was no need to rush.

"Prince Ferrand," she greeted him, nodding politely to the footman who pulled out her chair—another unnecessary servant in Ferrand's opinion.

"Princess," he greeted her in return.

When they were both seated, the footman served the meal, a savory fish and herbs dish, with boiled potatoes and seasoned vegetables. It was simple yet delicious food. Princess Marya seemed to enjoy it. He worried, having never traveled extensively before, that the simple fare would disappoint her. Life aboard a ship, it appeared, suited Princess Marya well. Another point in her favor.

"Have you been well?" he asked. "I know some do not have the stomach for sea travel."

"Yes. I am quite well," Marya replied.

"That is a relief. If you do get queasy, the cook can get you some ginger tea."

"Thank you," she replied. "And thank you for your comfort earlier. It has been a long several weeks for me."

"Of course." He longed to offer further words of soothing, but he held back.

An awkward silence descended, only the quiet sounds of polite dining permeated the air.

"How long have you captained this ship?" Marya finally asked.

"I think it has been approximately thirty years," he replied, offering no more.

He registered a look of surprise on the princess's face.

She opened her mouth as if to ask for further clarification but closed it again. Ferrand suspected she had been attempting to calculate his age. His age often surprised humans. His appearance had changed little since he reached adulthood around seventy years ago. No one knew quite how long a demi-fae's lifespan would be, but if they died of natural causes, it was always much longer than a human's lifespan.

"So, tell me about your kingdom," Marya prodded. The hopeful look on her face was almost too much for Ferrand.

"There is not much to tell. It is a standard kingdom. I have already told you I am not overly involved in its affairs." Marya's face fell, and Ferrand bit his tongue to keep from apologizing. It seemed he did not know how to have a normal platonic conversation without sounding so detached. Ferrand looked at his plate.

"The fish is delicious," Marya said. Ferrand could hear a forced lightness in her voice. She was trying so hard to make this dinner feel normal. They had spoken so easily at the ball. There must be a way to have a friendly conversation with her.

"I wanted to discuss the arrangements for our marriage," he changed the subject.

"Of course." She let out a lengthy sigh.

Ferrand pretended not to hear and continued, "My step-mother is eager to plan a grand affair. Do not let her bully you into anything. It is alright to take our time. And when the day has come and gone. Please don't feel pressured to jump into anything. As you have said, I am practically a stranger. Our marriage will be merely one of convenience. I think we can become friends in time, but I do not want you to feel pressured into anything further."

For the smallest breath, he could see the disappointment on her face, but she maintained her composure.

"Yes, of course," she replied. "Though I do hope you plan to keep good on your end of our bargain to take me traveling with you." She glared at him in an almost accusatory manner as if she expected him to go back on his word.

Why had he said that? That one seemingly insignificant comment would haunt him. If one day of sailing with her were any indication, it would be a test of willpower to keep his feelings in check.

"Or was that just a convenient way to get my agreement?" Her pleasant smile wavered the tiniest fraction. By the way she emphasized the word 'convenient,' he knew that she was throwing his own words back in his face, and she was displeased with the arrangement he was offering. Why was she suddenly bothered by it? She had said herself it was a political contract and nothing more.

"Of course, we can travel. Where would you like to visit first?" He would keep his word even if it would most likely cost him his sanity.

"As I've traveled nowhere before, it will all be new and exciting. Maybe someplace with warm sandy beaches. I would love to run, barefoot, along the shore." She had such an expressive face, from disappointment to excitement in a single breath.

The image appeared in his mind: Princess Marya running at her top speed, with her hair whipping behind her, barefoot in the sand. The salty spray from the waves would coat her in glistening drops of water. Ferrand swallowed hard, a rush of heat flooding his body. He would have to assign her a bodyguard so she could engage in such frivolity out of his sight.

Then he thought about another man watching her play in the ocean waves, and he wanted to tear the throat from the fictitious bodyguard. Skies, he needed to get her out of his head.

"Well, Princess, I will think of someplace warm and sandy to take you. But for tonight, I am exhausted. I think I will retire for the evening." He leaped to his feet, needing to be away from her at once.

Princess Marya could not contain her startled expression this time. She watched him exit—mouth agape. And for the second time that day, he hated himself for leaving her alone and confused.

Ferrand stormed up to the uppermost deck of the ship, tore off his shirt, and took to the sky, wings sprouting as he jumped. The crew was used to his wings by now, and they paid him no heed as he flew up to the upper crow's nest of the tallest sail post. He perched on the small platform, watching the dark sea below and wondering how he would ever get ahold of himself.

Geri, he noticed, perched on another mast nearby.

What am I going to do about Princess Marya? he asked his faithful companion.

Like Princess. Princess nice. Geri responded. Of course, she liked her. The princess was damned near perfect.

FERRAND DID NOT GO to his crew. They were perfectly capable of running the ship with or without his supervision. He loved being on the ship, but he knew that sometimes he was more of a figurehead than an actual sea captain. He had the respect of his men. However, other than Jacobe and maybe Ash, he could tell their respect existed because he was their prince, and not because of his skills as a captain.

Ferrand made his way to the solace of his cabin. The captain's quarters were the largest of the sleeping quarters, and they were quite comfortable. He preferred them to his suite at the palace.

His valet greeted him upon entering the room. "Good afternoon, Your Highness."

"Leblanc," he greeted the servant. Leblanc was relatively new to him.

The disadvantage of keeping a human staff when one's lifespan was more than double that of theirs was the constant need to train new servants. Ferrand didn't even see the need to have his own man, but his father had insisted that they would run their kingdom in the way of the humans. Because the portals to the fae realm had closed during the last war, his father worried about what would happen to their lineage over time. Would humans still respect them if they were less powerful?

His father suspected they would—only if they assimilated into their culture.

Ferrand grew up in the human realm, so he was used to it. He still did not see a need for a servant for every minor thing. He could dress himself. But he minded his father's wishes in this respect. He had to choose his battles where the king was concerned.

"Is there anything I can do for you, Your Highness?" Leblanc asked.

"No, thank you, sir. Go have yourself a break. I plan to rest for a bit."

"Yes, sir," Leblanc said, taking the dismissal for what it was and leaving Ferrand to himself.

Ferrand stretched himself out on the feather mattress to contemplate his dilemma. On the one hand, Princess Marya would make an ideal wife. She was intelligent, unlike most of the simpering humans in his court. She was adventurous, or so it seemed based on her initial excitement at the thought of traveling. She was beautiful, not that it would have mattered if she were plain, but it didn't hurt to find her attractive. If Ferrand's reactions to her were any indication, they would have excellent physical chemistry. And she wanted him just as much. But she was human. He had no intention of falling in love with a human.

If he and Marya were to have children—which they would need to do to continue his family line—he would not want his children to see him as a bitter man like the man his father became after his mother's death. He would remind the princess they were in a strictly political arrangement. That was what they had agreed upon. He would keep his feelings in check. He had to.

VII

Marya

"Olga, where are you? Come and look at Anna," Marya laughed, calling to her sister.

Olga hurried from their playroom into Anna's room, where Marya and Anna awaited her. Olga joined the sisters in their giggles when she saw Anna's ridiculous costume. The three princesses had been playing a favorite game of theirs, "Traveling Carnival." The previous summer, a traveling carnival had come to Oolaiah, and their governess had taken them to see it. Ever since, the girls always joked that with their Gods' Gifts, they would make a traveling circus of their own.

Anna, of course, was to play the part of their fortune teller. To make her seem more mysterious, Marya had taken as many silk scarves as she could gather up and draped them all around her sister's tiny frame, even braiding one into her sister's long blonde hair. To complete her look, Marya had snuck into Mother's bedroom and borrowed a few necklaces, which she had draped around Anna's slender neck.

"I know!" Olga exclaimed, running back into the playing room. When she returned, she was holding her precious kohl art set. Olga loved to sketch and draw, and Mother and Father had bought her a set of kohl sticks in varying thicknesses. She sat Anna back down on the stool at her dressing table and set to work with her kohls.

Bending down in front of her sister, Olga took the thinnest kohl stick and carefully drew the symbol of the Raven Prince—a swirl that formed the raven's eye and swooped to the back of his head with a triangle in front for his beak—right on Anna's forehead. The black raven stood out, a stark contrast to Anna's milky skin.

When the girls had finished Anna's costume, they set to work on their own. Olga ran back to her room to change while Marya finished preparing in Anna's room.

As the eldest, Marya was the only one of them who was wearing corsets yet. She didn't always like wearing them, but it suited her fine for her part as the acrobat. She stripped down to her corset and bloomers, stealing back one of Anna's scarves. She wrapped it around her waist as a tiny skirt, akin to the one the acrobat she had watched at the carnival had worn. She remembered her shock at seeing the girl parade about in what she had seen as brightly colored underthings. She also remembered her mother's shock when she was being fitted by the seamstress for her first corset only a few months later, and she had asked for one with red and black stripes and a set of polka-dot bloomers to match. It disappointed Marya to learn that proper young princesses only wore white underclothes.

So, she settled for a brightly colored scarf over her plain white corset and bloomers. She set to work, pulling out the pretty hairstyle her maid had given her that morning. Borrowing Anna's hairbrush, Marya tugged through her curls until they were loose waves down her back. She ran a long fingernail from the front of her scalp down to the back, dividing it into two sections that she hoped were even. She could have had Anna check, but she liked to prove she could style her own hair without a maid or anyone to help her. Holding one half of her hair in one hand and the silver brush in the other, she yanked the handful of hair up until she held it near the crown of her head. She tied it there with a ribbon, leaving a long tail on the side of her head. She did the same thing to the other side, smiling at what she thought was the most adorable hairstyle she had ever seen. It had also disappointed her to learn that the cute "pig-tails," as her governess had called them, were also something princesses did not wear.

Satisfied that she looked every bit as cute as the acrobat from the carnival, Marya rushed back into the playroom. Olga was still dressing, but Anna was setting up their small table as her psychic's booth.

Marya stretched two hands above her head and curved her spine into the shape of a half-moon, stretching while she waited for her sisters to prepare.

"I say, Marya," Ivan spoke from where he was sitting on the sofa with a book. "I don't think you should be doing that—and in your undergarments! It is not proper, and Anya will have a fit when she sees you."

"Anya is on holiday," Marya replied, not even bothering to argue whether it was proper. "Besides, she taught me how to stretch like this. It helps when I can't go running."

Ivan rolled his eyes and returned to his book.

Olga emerged from her bedroom in a bright green skirt that she had put over a long-sleeved nightdress. The way the dress puckered at the waist of her skirt and cuffed at her wrists looked almost like the fancy shirts that men wore under their jackets or a vest.

"Ivan. Can I borrow one of your vests?" Olga asked.

"Whatever for?" Ivan asked.

"I am trying to dress like a man," she replied.

"That is ridiculous," he said at the same time, Marya said, "That is perfect!"

"What is perfect?" Anna asked, turning to face them.

"Well, you've always got a Strong Man at the carnival. Whoever heard of a Strong Woman?"

The three girls giggled. Ivan rolled his eyes and went back to reading his book—a dull tome about the Great Fae War.

"Fine. Ivan, may I go get a vest from your room?" Marya asked.

"Mm-hmm," Ivan mumbled without looking up at her. Marya took that as a yes and skipped out of the room.

Only when she exited the playroom, she found herself not in the hallway but outside the palace. One of their golden carriages was waiting out front. Her father sat inside. His dark wavy hair was slicked back, and his golden crown rested atop his head—a heavy, wide circle with an owl emblazoned on the front with two shiny purple gemstones for eyes. He typically only wore it when going on official business.

A tall footman was waiting outside the carriage in his purple velvet leggings and black tunic, the official livery of the Sova family. He waited with the carriage door open. Marya realized she was the only one outside. He must be waiting for her. Marya skipped to the carriage and climbed in without letting the footman assist her. Her father raised an eyebrow at her. Not precisely a reproach, but a signal that he had noticed, and that he knew she knew better.

Marya refused to duck her head in apology.

The carriage rolled down the long road from their palace into the city proper. Marya loved going into the city with her father. She knew he was a good king. All of Selmy Island loved him. He made trips into the city of Oolaiah at least once every month. Marya knew the routine. First, they would visit the temple of Oola, the Owl Queen, Goddess of Wisdom and Knowledge. She was the matron goddess of their kingdom. They would pray to her for continued wisdom in guiding their people to prosperity.

Their family had their own chapel in the palace, with relics to all the gods of the Aviary. But it was customary for the sovereign to visit her temple. Marya bounced in her seat as they pulled up outside the worn stone building. Marya loved the temple. The rows and rows of candles that lined the beams that crossed the ceiling flickered in the ever-drafty old building.

Marya curtsied, placing three fingers to her temple. It was customary as she crossed the threshold. She was disappointed to note that because of the cloudy weather, the stained-glass windows were dull compared to a sunny day. The three windows depicted Oola in her three forms—to Marya's left, she was an owl, straight ahead a winged maiden with owl talons where legs should be, and to her right, a finely dressed woman. The scripture spoke of Oola's and all the gods' ability to transform between the image of a human and a bird with various stages of in between.

Under each window was a corresponding statue. Marya's father preferred to make his prayers at the owl, while Marya preferred the Human-like version of her goddess. She did not feel a powerful connection to Oola the way her father did. Maybe it was because of her Blessing from Otreus. He was jealous of his brother's marriage to queen Oola, having coveted her himself. Often, when she prayed at the statue, as she did then, she only pretended to pray. Instead she imagined herself as Queen Oola wise and strong with Otreus and Besmertnyy both in love with her. Oola ultimately chose Besmertnyy, but according to the version of the scripture preached in Selmy, she was the true leader of the Aviary, not Besmertnyy. Marya liked the idea that a woman could be the one in charge.

After enough time passed for Marya's father to believe she had made her prayers, she skipped across the temple to where he kneeled in front of the owl. She placed a hand on his shoulder and waited patiently for him to stand.

"Father?" she asked.

"Marya."

"Who replaces all the candles when they burn out?"

"Ever the inquisitive child. Your mind is sharp. An excellent trait in a Sova."

Marya rolled her eyes. Adults always said things like that. Marya knew she was smart. She and her siblings were all smart. It was just a fact, same as saying her hair was brown. She wanted praise for the things that made her uniquely her, the ones that set her apart from her family.

"All right. Well, who replaces the candles?" she asked again.

"I suppose one of the young acolytes of the temple."

"And where do they get the candles from? Are the priests and priestesses also candle makers?"

"No. I am sure one or many of the chandlers in the city donate candles to the temple."

"Donate means they just give them the candles without getting paid?"

"Yes, Marya. It is a great honor to provide for the temples." her father replied.

"But does that mean those businesses make less money than the ones who do not have the honor?"

"Probably not. Most likely, people will want to purchase from a shop that is so honored."

"So, they can charge more money for their other candles because people want their candles more?" she asked.

"My, you have an excellent head for economics," Her father commented. "You will make a magnificent queen someday, my pet."

Marya smiled and skipped back out of the temple with her father right behind her.

As before, she did not go through the door to the place she expected. Now she found herself on a balcony of her castle, facing out to the ocean. There was a large fleet of ships heading around the peninsula of Oolaiah. They must have been exiting the port on the eastern side of the island and heading around to sail west. Marya turned to the west to watch them leave.

Her eyes traveled over the ships that were reaching almost as far as she could see. Her gaze continued up from the horizon line, and it startled her to see the sky was growing dark even though the sun still shone behind her to the east. The sky grew darker, and it looked almost like a large cloud sweeping in, but it was an inky blackness rather than the familiar dreary grey of any storm she had witnessed. The black cloud grew and grew until it overtook the ships which disappeared into the darkness.

Marya shivered as she realized how cold she had become. The black cloud was approaching faster now, overtaking the entire fleet, and almost reaching the palace. Marya knew she should go inside, but she froze in place. Her feet were stone. The darkness swept down from above her; she opened her mouth to scream. The blackness was about to engulf her—

MARYA JOLTED AWAKE, clamping her mouth shut against the scream that had burst from her throat. Panic overtook her when she did not recognize her surroundings. The ground beneath her swayed. Marya thought she would be sick. She took a deep gulping breath, trying to steady the swaying.

She looked around the tiny room again. There was so much dark wood—the ornate, built-in wardrobe, the curved sleigh bed, a small writing desk, and a chair. The ship. She was on Prince Ferrand's ship. The swaying was the rocking of the boat on the ocean waves. She was still shivering. The covers from her bed had fallen to the floor.

Her door burst opened, and Prince Ferrand was standing there, a hulking silhouette illuminated by the moonlight.

"Are you all right?" he asked. "Where is your maid?"

Marya was shaking. She pulled her legs tight to her body. "She is probably asleep," Marya replied. "I- I am fine. It was just a nightmare." She couldn't stop shivering. Ferrand must have noticed because before she could get up to retrieve her fallen blankets, he was wrapping them around her. She scrunched herself into a ball and huddled in the sheets. The prince sat down on the bed next to her.

He wrapped his arm around her like her mother had when she was a small child. Why was he acting so kind? This man was the most confusing person she had ever met. One minute he was gentle and seemed to care for her. The next, he was completely ignoring her and speaking of marriages of convenience. What did he want from her?

"Do you want to tell me about it?" He asked.

Marya shook her head. She didn't want to talk about her family, and she wasn't even sure what to say about the other part of the dream. Ferrand pulled her closer, and she realized this was the first time that they were utterly alone—in her bedroom of all places. Marya swallowed. Her pulse quickened, and a slow tingling heat crept over her. Not necessarily an unwelcome sensation. It was not unlike the desire she felt when she wanted to run—only it wasn't centered in her legs. It was—oh gods. Her face heated.

Ferrand stiffened beneath her. Did he know the direction her mind had taken? Or had he also just realized how close they were? She could hear his heart beating with her head against his chest. It was picking up tempo, and her own was matching it. Marya closed her eyes and breathed deeply. Ferrand's scent filled her nose, the smell of the salty air, mixed with something else, almost like sweat, but earthier and not at all unpleasant. It fueled the fire that had started in her veins.

Marya pulled back from him and looked up at his face. He had a strong, somewhat angular jaw. His skin looked smooth as porcelain. No sign of stubble grazed his face, and she wondered if it was a Fae thing. Marya traced the line of his jaw with her eyes. She had the strangest desire to kiss the smooth, hard line. She tilted her head up towards him, just as he looked down at her, bringing his lips into the path of her gaze. Marya's lips parted, as if out of her control, their breath mingling together.

His face drew closer, and a faint fluttering started in her belly. He was going to kiss her. And she was going to let him. But then, just as it seemed their lips could not get any closer without touching, he changed his course, jolting upright and planting a kiss on the top of her head. A kiss her brother might have given her if he found her awake from a nightmare. Marya wanted to scream. Did he want her or not?

Ferrand stood, and she felt the absence of his body heat immediately. The chill returned, and she shivered again. Ferrand tucked the quilt tighter around her, but he did not return to her side. Without a word, he was gone. And Marya bit her tongue to stop herself crying out in frustration.

VIII

Ferrand

"**P**rince Ferrand!"

Ferrand turned to find his first mate calling to him. "Jacobe," he replied.

"Yer lady. You should keep an eye on her. She spends all day peppering the crew with questions about the ship. They don't know what to make of her. I think half the lads think themselves in love with the lass, and the other half- Well, you do not want to know what I think the other half is thinking about her."

Ferrand groaned. "What questions?"

"Well, if she were a lad, I'd have half a mind to hire her as a cabin boy. She seems fit, t'learn the ways of sailing."

That did not surprise Ferrand at all. One thing he found fascinating about Princess Marya was her desire to do anything the men around her could do, as well—sometimes better—than they could. It seemed the crew found her just as fascinating as he did. That was probably not good. They knew she was off-limits. He was positive they would do nothing to harm his princess. His princess? When had he started to think of her as his princess?

"Thank you, Jacobe. I will find her and speak to her."

"It might not be my place, yer highness-" Jacobe stopped.

"That's never stopped you before. Let's hear it," he prompted his first mate. He knew he outranked these men by leaps and bounds, but he had always asked them to treat him like any other ship captain, and that included advice from his first mate.

"Well, seeing as how she's yer intended, maybe you oughtta be the one to teach her what she wants to learn. I can't help but notice you haven't spent much time with the girl. If yer to marry her, you might wish to-"

"Your right, Jacobe," Ferrand interrupted. "That really is not your place. I will speak to her."

"Of course, Yer Highness," Jacobe replied. Ferrand hoped that Jacobe's sarcastic tone meant that he wasn't annoyed. Jacobe was the closest thing he had to a friend, but they weren't that close. Jacobe confided in him from time to time, but Ferrand didn't like to get close to his crew, or any of the humans for that matter. Their lifespans were just too short.

He knew, though, that what Jacobe said was true. Ferrand had spent little time with Princess Marya—not since her nightmare when he had been a heartbeat away from leaning down and kissing her. Just the memory of it had his lips tingling. He had gotten close enough to feel her breath before he thought better of it and kissed her on the forehead instead.

That had been three days ago.

Ferrand made his way across the ship, searching for his future bride.

It was easy to find her. When he reached the stern of the ship, he found all his off-duty men standing together in a huddle gawking—at his princess!

He didn't blame them. The sight of his fiancée contorting herself in what seemed like an impossible position! She was on her knees on the deck., her back arched so that her head almost touched the floor behind her. Ferrand swallowed. No wonder she had his men captivated. Ferrand let his eyes rove over her body. The curve of her—

Ferrand could have watched her all day, but he certainly did not want his men doing the same!

"Princess," he called to her.

Marya jumped at his voice, leaping to her feet and turning to face him. To his relief, the spell she had cast on his men was broken. They rushed to make themselves busy.

"Prince Ferrand," she greeted him. He noted that her voice shook slightly, and her cheeks colored.

"It has been brought to my attention that you are quite curious to learn about sailing. Jacobe says that you are full of questions. I did not realize you were so eager to learn the ways of a sailor."

"Yes. Well, you would not know that, would you?" she asked. "You haven't bothered to spend any time in my company these past few days." Her voice remained calm, but her expressive eyes betrayed her hurt.

Ferrand knew he should apologize. He wanted to, but it would be easier to keep her angry at him.

"Well, what is it you would like to know?" he asked.

Marya opened her mouth as if to answer and then closed it again. She bit her lip in that habit of hers that sent heat coursing through his body. Ferrand couldn't help the way his gaze lingered on her mouth. He licked his own lips. Why did the woman he was determined not to fall in love with have to be so damned attractive?

Marya's green eyes flared. "I would like to know why the ship's captain is staring at me like that," she finally responded.

Ferrand was unsure what to say. Did she not know the effect she had on him? The effect she was having on his men?

"Princess," Ferrand said through gritted teeth. "Please, I have a ship to sail, and a crew to command. If there is nothing you wanted to ask me, then I will be going. Also, you might want to think about where you are doing your- stretching or whatever it is you were doing. Half my men are too busy watching you to attend to their duties," Ferrand snapped.

That got her attention. Marya's eyes widened, and her faced flushed.

"Well, maybe if I had something to do all day long, I would not need to occupy my time stretching and questioning the crew," she shouted.

Ferrand could think of a few ways he would have liked to occupy her time. He tried to think of something to say that would not betray his thoughts.

"I am sorry, Prince Ferrand," she whispered before he had had a chance to answer. She was looking down at the floor now. "It will not happen again." And she fled, returning to the interior of the ship, presumably to her rooms.

Ferrand leaned against a pillar behind him, shaking his head and wondering what he would do about her.

RAND. RAND! Geri's voice was in his head. *Storm coming.*

A storm? Ferrand could usually predict a coming storm. He could feel the change in the air pressure before most people could. How had he missed it?

He needed to find Jacobe and plan with the crew.

"Your Highness!"

Ferrand turned around.

"Jacobe," Ferrand greeted him. "I was just coming to find you."

"It seems a storm is upon us," Jacobe replied. Ferrand tried to figure out how he had missed it.

"Aye. Go sound the alert. It will be all hands on deck, I am afraid. I will meet you at the helm. Let me just warn the princess she had better remain below decks for the time being."

Ferrand looked to the west, where the sun was sinking lower. Marya would be heading to the dining room shortly. He would head her off and give her his warning.

Ferrand found Marya just exiting her cabin.

"Princess Marya," he greeted her. "We are expecting a storm this evening. I cannot join you for dinner. It would be best if you remained indoors until the storm passes. And I would recommend asking a footman at dinner, to have the cook send some of that ginger tea I mentioned to your rooms. The rougher water can turn even the most hardened sailor's stomach."

"Will you miss dinner completely?" she asked.

"It is probable. I will eat in the mess with the crew later. Everyone will be hungry after navigating the storm."

"Prince Ferrand," Marya said.

"Yes, Princess?"

"Be careful, all right?" She surprised him by reaching for his hand and giving it a slight squeeze.

Her touch was warm. Ferrand smiled. "Thank you."

The pressure of her soft touch lingered as Ferrand made his way back to the weather decks to assist his crew through the storm. Ferrand and this crew had not weathered many storms together. Typically, he could predict them with more notice, and find a way for them to avoid the worst of the weather. This time would not be as lucky. Ferrand's men were skilled, however, and they were already running about preparing. His men were quick, scrambling up and down masts and adjusting the rigging.

"All right, Yer Highness, what's our strategy?" Jacobe asked when Ferrand reached the helm.

"There is no telling how big the storm is," Ferrand replied. "And with it coming from the east, we will have to cross it, eventually. How far are we from the southern borders of Wendyl?"

"We aren't too far off, highness, but the southern mountains of Wendyl make for a dangerous area in a storm. If we lose control, we could easily be washed up on the stones."

"There is that one cove, Swan's Bay, with the mountains on three sides. They would protect us from the brunt of the storm."

"It's too far east, Yer Highness. I do not believe we would make it there before the storm. We would still be sailing through it."

"But if we reached it quick enough, we might hunker down for most of it."

"Can we make it there? Would it be better to head South and go around the storm?" Jacobe asked.

"We do not know how far to the south the storm extends. We could still run out of time trying to skirt it, and then we will face it for an indeterminable amount of time. If we head for the cove, we will be more sheltered, and at least we will have a destination in mind." What Ferrand did not add was that hugging the coast would keep them from going much further off course—which would mean mean not adding too much time to their trip. He was eager to reach Southshore and get out of such close quarters with his betrothed. Every time he saw her around the ship, he was finding it harder to push her away.

"Aye, Sir," Jacobe acquiesced.

"I'll man the wheel, Jacobe," Ferrand offered. "Geri can remain up in the masts to give me a better vantage point. If the storm reaches us before we make it to the cove, we will need extra power to push through the wind. Have the men drop all the main sails and raise the storm sails. Send whatever crew we can spare on deck down to the galley to row." Ferrand could already feel the wind picking up, coming from the east. He could push back some of it, but he did not have near enough to the level of power they would need to fight the storm. His wind senses were picking up the air patterns now, and he wondered, again, why he had not noticed the storm sooner.

"And send me a few lads to run messages," Ferrand added. Once he melded further into his link with Geri, he would not be able to see through his own eyes for a time, and he would need a man at his side to let him know if anything important was happening on the decks. If the storm were as loud as he was expecting, he would need someone else to run orders.

"Aye, Captain," Jacobe responded, running off to give Ferrand's commands.

Geri, Ferrand called. *I need you to get as high up as you can.* I will look through your eyes. Keep looking towards the East and focus on the incoming waves. I am going to attempt to steer us around the biggest ones and over the smallest ones.

Geri flew up to a high mast, and Ferrand prepared himself for the task ahead.

Relaxing his mind, Ferrand slipped inside of Geri's. While they spoke telepathically frequently, this was not something they attempted often. Ferrand fought a wave of nausea as it threw his equilibrium off balance. He could still sense the ship rocking beneath him, but his vision was Geri's swooping through the air. The two sensations did not match up, and Ferrand found himself thankful he had not yet eaten.

When Geri settled on a high mast, Ferrand took several deep breaths, settling his stomach enough to concentrate.

"Yer Highness," one of the younger men spoke, near where Ferrand knew his body was. The sound nearby his actual body helped to anchor him further into the reality of where his body stood. "Jac sent me to assist you. It's Ash, here, by the way, Highness."

Ash was an observant lad. He was an excellent choice to be Ferrand's eyes on the ground. Ferrand explained to him what sorts of things to watch for and how he could best be of service while Ferrand kept the ship going as best as he could. Through Geri's eyes, he could see they were getting closer to the storm, but he could also make out the break in the mountains that signaled where the cove would be. The storm had not yet overtaken it, but he was not sure if they could make it there before the storm did.

Another crewman appeared at Ferrand's other side, and he sent him to the rest of the crew with the message that they were to make as much haste as possible. The oarsmen would have to push themselves, and Ferrand summoned his power from within to redirect some wind to their aid.

The next hour was a blur. The waves grew steadily larger as they made their way east at what felt like a crawl. Ferrand fought with all the strength he had to steer the ship away from the biggest waves and keep them on course for the cove. He was draining his mental strength as well, keeping the link between himself and Geri open to its fullest capacity. There was no point in using any more energy on the air. The measly amount of control he had over it did nothing against the large gusts that the storm brought.

When the rain, at last, started pounding them, they were almost to the cove. Rounding the rocky mountain that marked its entrance would be the most difficult trial yet. Ferrand called commands to his runners, unsure if they heard him over the raging storm. He counted on Ash to let him know if they needed anything else, but the boy remained quiet.

When they had finally rounded the bend, Ferrand felt his energy fading fast. He clung to wheel, the muscles in his arms and shoulders screaming in protest as he fought to keep them away from the rocky pass. They were just nearing safety when Ferrand's vision jolted back to his own. The suddenness of the return caused him to lose his grip on the wheel and stumble backward.

Without being asked, Ash was on the wheel, keeping them steady on course. Ferrand righted himself and made to take the wheel back.

"We're passed the worst, Highness," Ash shouted over the wind. "With all due respect, you look ready to collapse. We've got it from here." Ferrand looked around and noticed for the first time that several of his men stood around him. They nodded in agreement.

Ferrand was about to protest when he heard a shrill voice yelling his name.

Princess Marya waited just inside the doorway to the interior deck. She yelled his name again.

His first mate nodded at him again, and he took off towards her, wondering what she was doing. As he ran, he realized how stiff his legs were. He had been standing in one spot fighting the wind for far too long. He was halfway to where the princess stood when his knees buckled beneath him. The last thing he remembered was the sight of

Marya rushing out towards him, carrying a plate of food, and the rain soaking her from head to toe.

WHEN FERRAND WOKE, he first became aware that he was lying on his back. But the ground below him was not hard like the deck of the ship. It was soft. And it was not raining. He opened his eyes slowly, the wooden panels of the ceiling gradually came into focus. He was in his cabin.

With his heightened sense of smell, Ferrand scented the sweet smell of the princess before he saw her. He had no recollection of how he had come to be in his bunk, but the notion that the Marya was in his cabin where he was lying in his bed had him feeling hot. Ferrand attempted to sit up before realizing the splitting headache that was throbbing in his temples. Dizziness overtook him, and he quickly lay back down.

"Oh!" Marya gasped somewhere to his left. "You're awake!"

Ferrand heard the rustle of her clothing and the scrape of the chair she must have been sitting in. He felt her presence coming closer.

"What happened?" he croaked. His voice was hoarse, probably from shouting over the storm.

"Best we can guess is you over-exerted yourself. Your first mate mentioned that you were using enormous amounts of magic and physical strength to navigate the storm. It most likely drained all of your energy."

"Geri!" Ferrand exclaimed, remembering the moment when he had lost contact with her.

"She is fine. She has been pacing the decks in what we can only assume is anxious worry about you."

Ferrand nodded. He had never pushed their bond so far before. He knew it was draining. When he ran out of the mental strength to keep it going, it must have just stopped.

Marya was at his side now.

"You should eat something," she said. "Here, let me help you sit up."

Ferrand leaned into her touch when she placed one hand under his elbow and slid another one under him where his shoulders were resting on the pillows.

Ferrand bit down a groan. His muscles ached with the effort of sitting up. He fought the bile rising in his throat as a fresh wave of nausea overcame him. Marya must have noticed because she reached for a nearby bucket. Ferrand waved her off as his equilibrium returned.

Ferrand scooted himself back against the wall behind him. Marya turned towards the table where a tray of food was waiting, but he grabbed her hand to stop her. "What were you doing up on the decks in the middle of a storm?" he asked.

"I- I started to feel sick like you thought I might, so I was heading to the kitchen for some tea. I- I thought you might be hungry since you missed dinner. I thought I would bring something up for you. Then, of course, I saw how busy you were. I- I couldn't look away. You were like- I don't even know. I have never seen anything like it."

She was staring at him with a look of awe on her face. For the first time in his life, Ferrand thought he might blush. No one had ever looked at him with that level of amazement before.

Ferrand realized he was still holding onto her hand. He caught her gaze, and his heartbeat quickened. Marya opened her mouth to speak, and Ferrand's eyes drifted towards her mouth. He could easily close the gap between them. She was so close.

"Oh! I'm so sorry."

Marya jumped back from him, and Ferrand whipped his head around towards the door. How had he missed the sound of it opening? His usually keen senses were dwindling. First, he missed the warning of the storm. Now, he was missing out on sounds.

"I didn't mean to-" The young sailor, Ash, was standing in the doorway. "I was just coming to- Your bird, Highness. She's making the sailors anxious with her pacing. I was coming to see if- I'll let her know you're awake. She can hear me if I talk to her?"

The poor lad looked as if he had walked in on his parents in the act. Ferrand chuckled. "Yes. She can."

He ducked out of the room quickly.

"Well, now that you're awake. I should also-" Marya trailed off. She glanced at the door and back at him.

She was waiting for him to invite her to stay. He could see it in her eyes. He swallowed. If he let her stay- No, he couldn't let her stay. So what, if she had sat by his bedside while he slept? He needed to keep her out.

He nodded his head.

"All right then," Ferrand said. "Thank you."

Marya's face fell. She nodded and rushed out of the room.

Ferrand closed his eyes, leaning back against the headboard. He would not let himself become attached to her. He would not turn out like his father. The memory of his father, after his mother died, was one that would haunt him. Ferrand had never been close to him, but it only got worse after losing his mother. His father criticized everything he did. Ferrand had been a young man at the time. He was old enough. He did not need his father anymore, but still young enough to want his approval and his love.

That was why he could not let himself fall for her. He did not want to become his father. If—no, when—he and Marya had children someday, he wanted to be the kind of father that he had not had. His marriage to the princess was a political union and nothing more. Maybe if he kept telling himself those things, it would remain true.

IX

Marya

After the Prince's abrupt departure from dinner, their first night, and his strange behavior after her nightmare, Marya did not know what to think. But then there was the almost kiss after the storm. Marya's head was spinning, trying to figure him out. One minute she was in a strictly political marriage, the next it seemed like he wanted her. And to make it worse, she didn't even know what she wanted. She had wanted a political arrangement, but every time he did something kind or made her think he found her attractive, she found herself wondering what it would be like if they could have more.

Marya tried to forget about Prince Ferrand and enjoy her time on the ship. She had never even left her kingdom before, and she wanted to enjoy her trip. She tried to focus on that and not the confusion of her upcoming marriage.

She found that she enjoyed standing on the weather decks and looking out at the endless horizon. She itched to go for a run. She could almost replicate the feeling by standing at the front of the ship and letting the wind rush past her as they sailed. It did not settle her in the same way. In fact, the salty spray washing over her left her feeling exhilarated and slightly sticky.

She had never considered a life of travel. She hoped her soon-to-be husband would keep to his word about that, but how would they get on together as traveling companions? Would it be the same awkward uncertainty?

She replayed all their interactions in her head from the past week, searching for understanding, and still could not figure out what he wanted from her.

Maybe she would just have to confront him about it. She had also implied she only wanted a marriage of convenience. Perhaps, like her, he was realizing he wanted more, but did not want to push her if she was uninterested. She would just have to tell him she wanted it. At least, she thought she did. She could not get the thought of his piercing stare and their near kisses out of her head. And he had been so kind to her. She wanted it to be like that again. It was nearly all she could think about.

But she had told him at the ball she was only after his political influence. She would have to tell him if she wanted more. She couldn't expect him to read her mind.

Her mother and father had been happy together. They never spoke of love, at least not in front of Marya, but Father had always seemed to value Mother's opinions. They laughed a lot, and whenever they had a ball, even after all the years that had passed, they would still dance together. Her heart constricted again at the thought of her parents. At least, they had left this world together. She could not imagine one of them without the other.

Would Marya be able to find something like that with Prince Ferrand? Probably not if she continued to ignore him.

So that evening, she had Ellie dress her a little nicer for dinner—not that Ellie didn't dress her well every night. But tonight, she put on one of her favorite gowns. It might have been a bit much for dinner on a ship. It was probably more suited to a formal dinner in the castle, but she wanted to look her best. She needed to regain the easiness they had felt chatting at the coronation ball. She would make sure he understood she was in it for more than politics—if he was.

When she arrived in the ship's dining room, the elegance of it still surprised her. She had always imagined the inner rooms of a sailing ship would be dark and uninviting, but the chandeliers and brightly colored wall hangings were lovely. The prince sat at the head of the table, and a place was set for her in the usual spot at the other end of the table.

Prince Ferrand stood at her entrance. "Good evening, Princess Marya. You look lovely this evening." He was so polite and formal with her. A footman was waiting to pull her chair out for her.

Marya smiled. "Thank you, my prince. You are also looking well." Her greeting was not much better. It was probably not a great start to her plan. Making a quick decision, she walked past the waiting footman to the chair at the prince's right. She pulled it out herself and sat, giving a meaningful look to the footman who rushed to move her place setting to her new seat. She almost laughed out loud at the bemused look on Prince Ferrand's face. The comical expression put her at ease for the first time in days. She thought back to their playful banter at the ball, and she tried to figure out how to regain that ease.

The footman adjusted her chair slightly and then removed himself back to his post by the wall. Marya turned towards him and thanked him with a smile and a nod. Three more footmen entered the room, carrying covered dishes. They entered almost immediately after she sat as if knowing by some magic that they were ready to eat.

She had been later than usual to dinner, and Prince Ferrand, she noticed, had waited for her to arrive before being served himself. Her betrothed had impeccable manners.

Marya smiled with genuine enthusiasm at the stewards as they lowered the dishes near her. They served some type of fish in a cream sauce with roasted vegetables and potatoes with perfectly crisped skin. Every meal on the ship had been delightful, filled with spices she was unfamiliar with, that caused her mouth to water in anticipation. She had assumed that meals on a ship would not be as high quality as she was used to, but each evening's meal seemed better than the last. Perhaps on other ships, the food would not be as exquisite, but she was on the personal ship of a prince. It should not have been such a shock that he had an excellent cook. She would have to remember to suggest negotiating spices into any new trade bargains that Ivan worked on. Her sisters would love the exotic flavors.

She thought she could get used to the life of travel on the Falcon's Kiss. She didn't feel as though she had sacrificed a single luxury. The only thing that would make it better would be true companionship with Prince Ferrand. Which was why she planned to talk to him, she reminded herself. What did one say to the man she would marry but knew almost nothing about?

When she could not figure out how to broach the subject of their marriage arrangement, Marya set to looking him over. She had already noted that he was handsome, but she had not truly let herself take in his appearance since the evening of the ball.

That night, he had worn his inky-black hair loose to his shoulders. Since they had boarded the ship, he had kept it tied back at the nape of his neck. She supposed, with the wind common on the upper decks, it was a more practical style. Marya wondered what it would be like to be the one to undo the ribbons, watching the silky strands fall around his face in a frame. She blushed, remembering the soft tickle of his hair on her fingers when they had been dancing.

With his hair pulled back, it exposed his ears. They were not fully pointed, like the depictions she had seen of some fae, though they hinted at his heritage with just the slightest bit of a point. If she had children with this man, she realized, they would inherit some of his fae blood. She blushed again, thinking about having children with him. Surely, they *would* have children someday which would mean—

Marya felt her face heating. On the evening before they had set sail, Aunt Leina, Tavar's wife, had shown up at her rooms to explain her marital obligations to her. Marya had known a little, but Aunt Leina had been thorough, if awkward, in her descriptions. Thoughts of future children sent her mind wandering to that conversation, and sparks of unfamiliar heat erupted in her body as she thought about the man sitting next to her, touching her bare skin.

What would it be like to have his firm hands roving over her body? She remembered her surprise at his calluses, not typical for a prince.

She realized now it was because of his time sailing his ship. She imagined their slight roughness traveling down the length of her stomach, leaving goosebumps in their wake until they got closer and closer to—

Marya almost gasped out loud. Stifling herself, she made a strange, strangled sound instead.

"Are you all right, Princess?" her betrothed's voice startled her back to reality. "You are looking flushed. Are you well?"

It did not surprise her to know her face was flushed the way her skin burned and tingled. The feeling was like the itch she got when she longed to run, to push her physical limits. What would it be like to push herself physically with this man? The weight of his large, muscled body pressing into her. Her face burned. What was wrong with her? "Yes, my Lord," she managed to squeak out as a reply. "I am fine."

She felt anything but fine. She wished she *could* go for a run. It always helped her relax. But being on a ship provided her with no place to release her energy. The anxious tingle she felt when she wanted to run crept in to join the other sensations she was having, and she wondered if her inability to do so could be, in part, why she had so quickly heated with desire.

Marya had rarely gone so long without burning off her excess energy. She chose, most mornings, to wake early and have a run while her sisters would lie about in their beds. She forced herself to take a few slow, steadying breaths, trying to calm herself down.

Ferrand was looking at her strangely. His blue eyes had darkened to the deep color of the sea under the night sky. His breathing seemed slightly tense. Had he known what she was thinking about? Marya willed herself not to blush again, continuing her deep breathing. As she relaxed, the prince seemed to, as well.

She couldn't quite calm the itch to run, but she returned herself to a more familiar level of discomfort at least.

"How have you been enjoying our travels?" he asked. His voice was slightly huskier than usual.

"The trip has been pleasant thus far. The open-air and the ocean all around us are quite lovely. Although, I do long for someplace to run. And now that stretching on the decks is out of the question..." She trailed off. She hadn't meant to sound accusatory. It wasn't his fault there was nowhere to run on the boat, or that stretching on the decks distracted his lecherous crew.

"I can imagine it has been difficult. I have heard the more *physical* Gods' Gifts can be demanding of use." Had he meant to emphasize the word physical like that? She knew she was blushing again, and the tingling returned straight to her core.

"I might be able to arrange something for you." He continued. "Meet me on the upper deck in a few hours."

What did he mean he could arrange something for her? They were on a boat. And it was getting late. She agreed to meet him out of sheer curiosity.

Marya never managed to bring the topic around to what sort of marriage they would have. She could not stop wondering about their midnight meeting. What surprise could Prince Ferrand possibly have in store for her?

X

Ferrand

Ferrand paced the compact space in his cabin. He was sure he was wearing a path in the worn wood planks. What had he been thinking to invite Princess Marya for a midnight meeting? That was definitely not keeping his distance. And that dinner. It had taken all his will to remain composed at the scent of her evident arousal. His keen senses had betrayed her thoughts as he felt her eyes roving over him.

It had been perfect timing on her part to mention running. Prince Ferrand knew that the ship would pass a small island off the southern coast of Wendyl. He had already planned with his crew that they would anchor nearby so he could get off and spend some time on the island that evening. When the princess expressed a desire to stretch her legs, the invitation had tumbled from his lips before he knew what he was saying.

So much for the peaceful night to himself that he had planned.

He brought to his mind the image of her running in the surf that he had been playing and replaying since it had first come to him, and he knew he would be a goner. Still, he was a man of his word, and he would not abandon her after making such a promise.

"Leblanc," he called to his manservant, who was waiting for direction.

"Yes, Your Highness," Leblanc replied.

"Please fetch me a flying tunic."

"Yes, Your Highness."

Ferrand rarely wore the flying tunics that his father had had specially designed for him. He did most of his flying without a shirt at all, but the air had a chill in it that late at night—and the idea of carrying the Princess against his bare chest was too much. Leblanc fished out a black silk garment from the wardrobe. It was a long silk tunic that fell almost to his knees. The front of the garment closely resembled a silk tunic that any of the human nobility might wear. It had a sharply pointed collar and silver buttons closing the deep opening. The back of the garment was where the key differences came in. The top and bottom third of the tunic attached to the front in a typical fashion, but long silk strips embroidered with silver swirls made up the middle third of the garment's back. Leblanc crisscrossed the pieces in such a fashion that a wide triangle on Ferrand's back remained exposed, wrapping the silk strips around his front to function also as the belt that would cinch the tunic at his waist. Leblanc wrapped the strips to cross once again in the back and tied them to loops sewn at his hips.

From the front, it might not even be apparent there was anything unique about the tunic. From the back, however, there was room for his wings to emerge. The tunic was his favorite style of flying garment, but he also had button-down shirts that he could wear under a jacket for more formal occasions. Princess Marya had not seen his wings yet. He paced again as he worried what she might think.

Leblanc finished by assisting him into a pair of dark green, form-fitting, leather trousers, retying his hair, and lacing his knee-high leather boots for him. Ferrand could have completed the entire ritual on his own, but he found his servants often got surly with him if he didn't let them do their jobs. When he was king, he would pay them all a handsome retirement salary and send off all but the most necessary servants.

Ferrand made his way to the top deck of the ship and waited for the princess to arrive.

Princess Marya met the prince on the upper deck at the prescribed time. He had not told her where they were going, but she had dressed appropriately in one of her more casual dresses, pale green with a floaty skirt and sturdy boots she could run in.

"Are you ready?" He asked.

"Ready for what?" Marya responded.

"You'll see." Prince Ferrand closed his eyes and stretched out his arms to either side of his body. He tried to unveil his wings in as dramatic a fashion as he could muster. No one—at least not in the human world—was sure what the physiology was that allowed many of the remaining demi-fae to summon and dispel their wings. It was some form of fae magic that lived in them. At around three or four years old, though he didn't remember it, they had just sprouted from his back one day. As a small child, he had no control over it. His father did not have access to wings, which had meant he had to learn to fly on his own. His half-brother Louis also had wings, and Ferrand had taught him to fly.

He opened his eyes, searching his future wife for a reaction. Her eyes were wide with what appeared to be a combination of surprise and awe. He held his breath, waiting for her to say or do something that would let him know what she really thought.

When she just stood there agape, he prompted her. "Well, what do you think?" There was a slight quiver to his voice that irritated him. What did it matter what she thought?

"They're lovely," she finally replied.

He had been hoping for "impressive" or "magnificent" or something, but the impressed stare she gave him told him that "lovely" might have been an understatement.

"They can—I mean you can—fly?" she asked breathlessly.

"Yes," he replied.

"I had no idea. Do all the—what do you call someone who is not a fae but has fae heritage?" she asked.

"Demi-fae. Though it is a bit of a misnomer as I am only one-quarter fae, not half. My father's father was a wind fae. He died during the Great Fae War. He fought against the Dark Fae to protect humans. He wanted to take my grandmother and father, who was young at the time, back to the fae realm, but he died. And then the

Gates closed. Luckily, my father also fell in love with a human woman. Twice, in fact. At least I think he loves my stepmother. He's not very forthcoming with his emotions." Why was he rambling? "Anyway, you were about to ask if all demi-fae have wings, I think."

Princess Marya nodded her head, still staring at him in a way that was making him uncomfortable. "Not all demi-fae have wings. No one is sure why some have them, and others do not. It seems to skip a generation. My father does not have wings, but my brother and I both do. Most likely, our children will not."

His betrothed's cheeks flushed. He was sure it was the mention of children that had done it. She was probably thinking about how they would go about getting children. The thought made him hot, as well, but he pushed it aside and changed the subject.

"I spoke to the captain. He altered our course a bit. We are close to a small island. I could take you there. To run. If you would like."

She beamed at him. Apparently, he had done the right thing.

"That would be fantastic. It's been difficult going so long without a proper run." Then she froze. "Would you be? I mean-"

"Yes, I will have to carry you. I promise it is very safe. I have carried more weight before. And I am an excellent flier."

He gestured for her to come closer and reached his arms out for her. She stepped towards him tentatively and let him pull her into his arms. This was the most physical contact they had shared since their first night on the ship when he had comforted her from her nightmare. Ferrand's heart thudded in his chest. He wondered if she could feel it. Her slender body fit perfectly against him, and he found he longed to enjoy the embrace. Ferrand inhaled the scent of her. Skies, she was growing aroused with his arms around her. What would it be like to give in to that passion? Ferrand felt himself growing hard at the thought.

Ferrand swallowed hard, willing himself to relax. The sooner they reached the island, the sooner he could put her down.

Ferrand held her closer, picking up her legs and cradling her against him. He lifted into the sky and felt her gasp and curl in closer against him. He loved flying, and he hoped she was enjoying it as much as he was.

The air was cool against his hot skin. He could have flown faster, but he did not want to scare Marya on her first flight.

WHEN THEY REACHED THE island, Ferrand set Marya down on the sandy beach.

"How did you like your first flight?" he asked.

She wobbled on her feet for a moment, but her voice was steady when she responded. "It was unlike anything I could have imagined."

"You were not afraid I would drop you into the ocean?"

"Of course not. I could tell that your arms were strong and safe around me." It was dark on the island, but Ferrand's eyes had adjusted enough during the flight to see in the ambient moonlight that her cheeks stained with color yet again. He felt the sudden urge to stretch his wings and preen. Skies Above, she was making a fool out of him.

They had landed on a narrow stretch of beach. It may not have been the warm, luxurious beach she had envisioned when she had talked about travelling to a beach to run. But it stretched out quite a bit to the east and west, and she could get herself running at full speed. To their north lay a bit of grass and stone which butted up to a rocky cliffside. Typically, when Ferrand visited the small island, he would fly up into the mountains, but for the Princess's run, he would make the sacrifice and remain on the beach.

"You can run by yourself if you would like. Or I could run with you. Well fly. I don't think my feet could keep up with your Gift, but I think my wings could do it. If you would like to be alone, though, I understand."

"You really think you could keep up with me?" she asked.

"I haven't seen you push yourself to the limits, but I assure you I can fly pretty fast."

"I'll start off slow for you," she teased, giving him a cheeky wink. "See if you can keep up."

Compared to most humans, Ferrand would not have called it slow when she took off. But he was faster. At that speed, he could probably have almost kept up on foot, but instead, he flew up above her and watched her from slightly behind. She was every bit as enchanting to watch as he had imagined. He could visibly see the tension in her body release as she moved. After a moment, she stopped and sat down on the sand.

Princess Marya surprised him by unlacing her boots and leaving them on the beach. Then she took off running faster than he imagined possible. She moved closer to the ocean, letting the waves crash over her bare feet as the hem of her flimsy dress dipped in the water. He was glad there was so little light, or the gown would probably be transparent.

Ferrand kept pace with her, flapping his wings yet keeping himself at a slight distance. He was enjoying the view quite a bit, but he wanted to prove he could keep up.

XI

Marya

Marya ran down the sandy beach, enjoying the feel of the cold water lapping against her ankles. She had felt hot all over after letting Ferrand carry her against his chest.

When he asked if he could run with her, she had almost said she preferred to run alone. But then, she realized, she had no idea if that was true, having known no one who could keep up with her. It was probably a good thing Prince Ferrand was not far off, as she was not used to running in the dark. The long flat beach was much easier to run in than her forest, however.

Behind her, the air pounded, and the sound of heavy wing beats filled her ears. Marya surged forward, excitement thrumming through her veins. She had never run with anyone before. Prince Ferrand had been keeping a slight distance between them, but she felt him closing in. He was almost on top of her. It startled her into a gasp when his large hands grabbed her waist. He lifted her up and into the air.

Ferrand held her below him, her arms outstretched. The only connection between them was where his hands gripped her slender waist. Her initial surprise quickly turned to delight. She threw out her arms to the sides. She almost felt like she was the one flying like this. It was better, even, than their first flight. The air rushing past her in great gusts from the prince's wings was exhilarating. She closed her eyes, reveling in what she was feeling. The tightness in her shoulders released, and the muscles in her arms and legs were loose for the first time since her parents' death.

CRACK!

A streak of lightning startled her out of her reverie. The entire sky lit up around them; a shaft of light stabbed downward into the ocean, much closer than she would have liked. The Prince's grip tightened on her waist, immediately shifting his position. His legs dropped downward, perpendicular to the ground, and he was back-winging hard against the air to slow them to a stop. He placed her onto the sand and dropped to the ground beside her.

And then the rain poured down on them.

Big heavy droplets fell from the sky, soaking them through in an instant.

"Come on!" Ferrand growled. He dragged her by the hand towards the cliffs, as another bolt shot down from the sky.

"I cannot risk flying us back in this storm. It is too dangerous. There must be a cave we can hide out in until it passes."

"Your men said the weather would be nice for the rest of the trip."

"I thought it would be, too. I would have never flown you out here had I known." They scrambled over rocks as they got closer to the cliff. Marya regretted leaving her boots behind as she scraped her feet along the stones. Ferrand pulled her arm harder until he finally ducked into a small opening in the rocks. She scurried in behind him.

"I am so sorry about this," he apologized. "I should have known."

"It's fine. I can rough it in a cave for a while if I have to."

"Such a brave young princess," he teased.

She shot him a look of annoyance, though she doubted he could see it in the darkness. She could only just barely make out the outline of his shadow.

"I am serious. Few young ladies would smile whilst standing in a black cave, dripping wet from head to toe."

Was she smiling? She had not even realized it. The feeling of flying, running, and being free had been so amazing that even soaking wet, hiding out in a cave, she could not bring herself to feel anything but happiness.

"And especially forced to hide away with a man she barely knows and does not want to marry," Prince Ferrand continued.

"That is not entirely true," she replied before she could stop herself. For the first time, she was confident that she did not hate the idea of marrying him. Still unsure of how he felt about her, she continued, "It was never about *you*. I had not thought to marry *anyone*." She could barely make out his features in the dark cave, but she thought his shoulders sagged a bit. Had he been hoping that she would say she wanted to marry him? Gods, he was a puzzle. She had never been good at puzzles. Sure, she was intelligent, but puzzles were intentionally tricky and misleading. She hated that feeling of uncertainty. Marya was used to being certain about everything she did.

But she did not feel that the prince was intentionally trying to trick her or mislead her. Maybe he was just as confused about what he felt as she was.

"You know," she said. "I had not thought to marry, but if I am going to marry anyone, I am glad it is you." The last words came out in one breath. She bit her lip nervously, waiting to hear what he would say.

"Yeah?" His voice was little more than a whisper.

She had decided that she would talk to him about their marriage arrangement. Trapped in a cave together in the middle of a thunderstorm seemed as good a time as any.

"You said the other night-"

"Forget what I said," he interrupted her. He pressed his finger to her lip to shush her.

Marya brushed his hand away. "No, let me finish. I want no more uncertainty between us. I want to say this, and I want to make sure we are in agreement. I need to know where we stand."

"All right." He nodded his head, encouraging her to continue.

"At dinner. The other night. You said that our marriage was only one of convenience. I know that is what we agreed to when you asked. But I am starting to wonder if, maybe, we could have something more."

A streak of lightning lit the sky outside the cave, and Marya saw his face more clearly. Everything she was feeling, the doubt, the hope, the desire, was mirrored on his stupidly handsome, perfect face.

"Yeah?" he asked.

Marya reached out and took one of his hands with her own. "Yeah," she said.

They stood like that for an indeterminate amount of time. Her heart raced.

Crack!

Another lightning bolt streaked outside, lighting up the inside of their little cave. Ferrand's hand was still clasping hers. He was looking down at her. His eyes were dark and stormy as the night outside the cave. His mouth hovered above her own. Nothing would interrupt them this time.

"Can I kiss you, Princess?" He asked. His voice was strained, and his breathing was uneven.

"Marya," she breathed. "You can call me Marya. We are to be husband and wife, after all."

"Can I kiss you, Marya?" He dragged out her name like it was a prayer, sending a shiver down her spine.

Words would not form. Marya nodded her response. She tilted her mouth up towards him, closing her eyes and waiting. She had never been kissed.

His lips were warm against her own. She was unsure what to do next, so she let Ferrand lead. He pulled her body closer, placing one hand on the small of her back and running his other hand through her damp hair. His fingers snagged in a few knots, and she chuckled against his mouth.

Marya had been cold from her wet clothes, but she was quickly growing warm. Ferrand prodded her lower lip with his tongue, and she let out a little gasp of surprise, opening her mouth to him. He swiped his tongue inside. The jolts of electricity it sent coursing through her body surprised her. She did her best to imitate what he was doing. He made a little humming sound that vibrated through both of their mouths. She assumed that meant he liked it and continued. This time, he groaned.

Ferrand pulled back from the kiss. He looked down at her with an expression that made her insides quiver. "Oh, Marya." He whispered. The lightning flashed outside the cave again. His gaze was fiery, his eyes penetrating. She could barely breathe.

And then she shivered.

His passionate gaze melted into concern. And once she started shivering, she could not stop. The moment had passed. She was cold and wet, and she longed for the warm comfort of her cabin on the ship.

"Come here, Marya." Ferrand grabbed her hand and led her further into the cave. He sat down on the floor stretching his legs out and gestured for her to sit between them.

Marya lowered herself down to sit, and he wrapped his large feathered wings around her. It surprised her how soft his feathers were. The outer feathers of his wings were damp, but underneath, they were warm and dry. Marya tried to relax into the warmth of him, but she continued to shiver.

"Marya, I know this will sound forward of me, but you need to remove your gown."

"I will not."

"The wet material is making you colder, and we have no way to dry it right now."

Marya looked at him with skepticism, but she knew he was probably right. There was no wood for a fire. Even if he went to find some, it would be wet.

"So, I am to stand here without any clothes?" she asked.

"I don't know if this will make you feel more or less comfortable," he replied. "But I will take off my clothes. We can generate some body heat between us. The storm won't last long. Summer thunderstorms are intense, yet short-lived."

Marya knew he was right. It was not as if he was asking to ravish her—though the thought sent another wave of heat over her. He was trying to keep them warm.

Marya stood to remove her gown. She reached around to the back where the laces held it shut. It tied right in the middle of her back, and she could not undo the laces herself. She wished she had worn a different gown, but how could she have known she would need to undress herself. Marya hated to ask for help for such a simple task. The thought of Prince Ferrand removing her dress had her trembling.

"I- I'm not sure I can undo the laces by myself," she whispered. Just thinking about it sent another flush of heat over her. Maybe she could just keep thinking of all the things he might do to her, and she would generate enough heat on her own.

She heard Ferrand moving closer to her. She held her breath as he inched towards her. She felt a tug at the laces, but his presence still seemed far. He must have been keeping as much space between them as possible to preserve her dignity. A few more tugs, and the laces sprung loose. She was not one to wear her garments so tight that she could not breathe like some other court ladies she knew, but still, her body relaxed as the tension on her dress released. She wiggled and shimmied, trying to loosen the gown the rest of the way, but the damp fabric clung to her skin.

Marya could hardly breathe when she felt the heat of him close in on her, and when Prince Ferrand's callused hands slid beneath the back of her gown, she thought she might faint. Slowly, he peeled the wet fabric away from her damp undergarments and her equally damp skin. His hands felt warm on her bare shoulders. He slid them down her arms, pulling the fabric of the dress down with them. The bodice of her dress fell forward.

Marya bit back a whimper when his feathers brushed first along her arms, and then lightly over her breast. She no longer felt cold at all. Her skin was an inferno. It was a wonder the last of the rain had not evaporated away. She wondered if Ferrand was burning up, as well.

Marya's heart raced, and she failed to stifle the next whimper as he let his hands glide from her underarms, down the side of her ribs, and to her hips, with nothing but the thin cotton of her chemise between his hands, and her sensitive skin. Feathers continued to flit over her skin with every movement he made. His hands stopped where the fabric had caught at her hips. He gave one more quick tug on the skirt, and the whole dress pooled at her feet, leaving her standing in just a chemise and bloomers. She was glad she had dressed simply. She could not imagine what would happen if he had to undo complicated petticoats or hoops.

She continued to face away from him, knowing that the dampness on her thin top would not hide her breasts.

She felt the warmth of him retreat. She avoided turning to look at him as she heard the soft hissing of his silk shirt sliding over his damp skin.

"Can I hold you again?" his voice cracked when he spoke. It relieved her to know she was not the only one affected by their current situation. "For warmth, I mean," he continued.

She nodded, hoping he could see the small movement in the dark. Ferrand pulled her back into his embrace without a word, but she felt him shiver as her cold, wet, undergarments pressed up against his bare skin.

"I- I can take this off, too," she whispered. "It will make it easier to warm up." She heard his breath hitch as she reached down to grab the hem of her chemise and pulled it off over her head, tossing it to the side. Next, she untied the drawstring on her bloomers and let them drop. She stepped out of the last of her clothing and kicked it to the side.

XII

Ferrand

Ferrand let out a low growl as he made out the silhouette of her bare backside. He wanted to grab her by the hips, pull her back against him, and take her right then. He should have turned away, but he was transfixed. He felt his arousal growing as she kicked all of her clothing out of the way and backed herself into his embrace.

He knew that this time when she leaned into him, she could feel his erection pressing into her backside. She was so young. How much did she understand about what went on between a man and a woman? The sharp intake of her breath confirmed that she was aware of his hardness.

"I'm sorry," he whispered as he wrapped his wings around them once more, hoping to keep her warm.

"For what?" She asked. "We are to be husband and wife before long. I assume this will not be the last time I feel your—you know." She laughed.

Not if he could help it. Skies above, he wanted to be with this woman as often as she would let him. He felt the vibrations of her laughter through his entire body. She giggled again and squirmed. He stifled another low moan as her bottom brushed across his erection.

"Your feathers are tickling me," she half moaned, half laughed.

"I'm sorry," he mumbled again.

"There is no need," she breathed. "It is well—it feels—" she gasped again, but Ferrand was fairly certain it was in pleasure this time. He tried to concentrate on where his feathers brushed against her. There was no feeling in his feathers, of course, but his wings were sensitive enough to feel each feather moving. He knew they were brushing across her bare breasts, and stomach, and her thighs, and possibly even—

Ferrand had never been with a woman while his wings were out before. He had avoided it, actually. He felt a thrill, knowing what they were doing to Marya.

He felt a noticeable difference in the way she was currently shivering compared to earlier. Small goosebumps erupted over her skin, yet she certainly was not cold. Their skin was molten, where their bodies pressed together. She made tiny breathy noises every time his wings shifted slightly. Skies above, he longed to run his hands across her the way his feathers were. He did not want to move too quickly for her, but he could not stand like a statue behind her until they were dry. He cautiously placed his hands on her hips. When she didn't protest, he slid them around her waist, pulling her tight against his abdomen, his erection pressing into her back.

She groaned, dropping her head back onto his shoulder. The scent of her arousal intoxicated him. Ferrand dipped his head down, placing a feather-light kiss on the spot where her neck and shoulder met. Her skin was on fire. His skin was on fire. The chilly dampness of the leather trousers he still wore was the only thing keeping him from burning alive.

"Ferrand," she gasped, squirming as he licked his way up her neck, placing a kiss on the spot right below her ear.

He moaned as she shifted against him.

"I don't really know a lot about, you know, what goes on between a man and a woman, but I can feel that you are, um, ready, and well—" she trailed off mid-sentence.

"You have no idea. You're so—oh Skies, Marya. I want more than just a political alliance too. I want all of it. All of you." At that moment, he wanted nothing more than to spend eternity holding her in his arms. Why had he denied himself?

She turned herself around in his arms and kissed him again. Their bodies melted together. Ferrand wanted to continue kissing her, but he needed to sit. He felt dizzy with lust, and his damp pants were chafing against his erection.

"Marya, would it be all right if I finished undressing?" he asked. "These pants are growing very uncomfortable."

"Oh!" she cried, jumping back from him. "Yes. Of course."

He chuckled when she turned away from him, presumably to give him privacy. He quickly divested himself of his boots and pants. The storm was still raging outside. They would have to find a way to get comfortable. Ferrand felt around on the cave wall for the smoothest spot. He sat down against the wall. The stone was like ice against his flaming skin.

"Come. Sit. I'll keep us warm."

Marya turned towards him. He felt her gaze roving from his head down his body. She bit her lip as her eyes stopped for the briefest of moments on his groin before continuing down his legs. How much could she see in the darkness of the cave?

He had expected her to sit with her back against him, but she surprised him by kneeling in the v of his legs. She pressed her hands against his chest, leaning upwards to capture his lips in another searing kiss. He moaned when she ran her hands from his chest down the length of him to settle on his hips. He slid his hands down her back, cupping her bottom in response.

Marya sighed into his mouth, and he took that as confirmation that she liked what he was doing. She slipped her arms around his neck, pressing her bare breasts against him. His erection was caught tightly between them, and he groaned into her mouth with every movement she made.

Marya tugged at the ribbon in his hair, and the mass of it swung forward, falling around them and brushing their shoulders. Marya hummed against his mouth as she ran her hands through the damp strands of his hair.

Ferrand nipped her bottom lip lightly, and she squirmed in his lap.

He stroked her legs, with long, languid strokes down to her knees and back up to her bottom, squeezing lightly. Marya kept one hand tangled in his hair, and the other one trailed down the column of his neck, over his shoulder, down his side. He closed his eyes in pleasure, leaning his head against the rock wall behind him.

Ferrand jumped in a start when she slid her hand between them and wrapped her hand around his erection.

"Sorry," she whispered.

"No- it's- I was just surprised. You have no idea what you're doing to me, Marya."

"I have some idea," she whispered. "If this feels as good as what you're doing to me, I mean."

"We should probably stop." He hated the words as they came out of his mouth, but he knew they were true.

"Why?" she breathed.

"It's not proper."

"I think we've passed the line of what is proper already."

"I know but—"

"I don't want you to stop touching me like this, Ferrand." Her tone was almost bossy. No female had ever taken that tone with him before, and it made him want to pounce on her.

"What else are we going to do while we wait out the storm?" she continued.

"Marya," he asked. "How much do you know about what goes on between a man and a woman?"

"I know how a child is conceived if that is what you are asking."

"Do you know that there are ways we can enjoy each other without risking a child out of wedlock?"

"Well, if it involves more of what we have been doing, please don't stop. I feel—I can't even explain it. I just know I need you to keep touching me."

Ferrand growled again. She would not need to tell him twice. He carefully laid her down on the ground. He wished he had a more comfortable place for them to do this. But she didn't complain. He wished he could see her face better, so he knew what she was thinking.

Ferrand lay on his side next to her, his wing pinned awkwardly behind him. He brushed his hand from her ribs to her hips and back up again. With each sweep, he drew closer and closer until his fingers met her wet heat. Marya bucked her hips in surprise, and Ferrand looked deep into her eyes, questioning if he should continue.

Marya met his gaze with a steady, heated gaze of her own. She licked her lips, and it was all he could do to hold himself back from taking her right there on the ground when he had just told her he would not. Instead, he slipped a finger into the wet heat of the folds between her legs. She arched beneath him, and he continued his ministrations. He brought the curve of his wing down around them, lightly brushing the feathers across her pert nipple.

The moan she let out was nearly enough to send him over the edge. His erection throbbed with need, but he ignored it, preferring to focus on Marya's pleasure. Ferrand leaned down and, again, took her mouth with his own. She writhed beneath him.

"More," she panted against his mouth. She was so hot and wet for him. Ferrand slipped a second finger inside her, pressing the heel of his hand against the sensitive spot at the top of her opening. Marya bucked her hips against his hand, and he did it again, enjoying the little noises of pleasure she made.

Ferrand shifted his weight so that he was above her. Never breaking contact between their mouths, Ferrand cupped her breast with his free hand. He dragged his thumb across her nipple, and she moaned again.

Ferrand moved his lips down her jawline and down her neck, licking and nipping the skin as he went. "Gods, Ferrand," she breathed out when he sucked on the juncture of her shoulder. Her body was taut beneath him. He knew she was close to her climax. Ferrand sucked and licked his way down her chest, stopping to savor her breasts. She arched against him when he sucked a nipple into his mouth.

Ferrand worked his fingers slowly in and out of her wet heat, dragging them up and around to swirl over her sensitive bundle of nerves before plunging them back inside. Several more times he did this, feeling her body stiffening beneath him, Ferrand pressed his lips back against hers. She thrust his tongue into his mouth, and he continued to pleasure her with his fingers.

He quickened the pace, stroking her over and over until, at last, her body shuddered, and she cried out his name. Quake after quake racked her delicate frame, but Ferrand did not stop until she lay spent on the floor.

"Oh gods, Ferrand," she whispered. He rolled back onto his side, pulling her close to him and kissing her hair. "Mmm," she murmured sleepily against his chest. Ferrand wrapped his wing around them, his own need forgotten as he held her tight, listening to her breathing as she drifted off into sleep in his arms.

AT SOME POINT, HE MUST have fallen asleep, Ferrand realized, as he slowly came to. Everything was quiet. The storm had stopped, and the cave was growing lighter. His back ached from sleeping on the stone floor, and his wings, still wrapped around Marya's sleeping form, were unused to being active for so long. Usually, he summoned them to fly and dispelled them when he finished. Ferrand arched his back and stretched. The movement seemed to stir Marya. She rolled off him sleepily, jolting awake when her bare leg touched the cold rock.

Ferrand stifled a laugh at the play of emotions running across her face—first confusion, then memory, then her pretty little cheeks colored bright red as she noticed their position.

"Good Morning, Princess," he murmured.

Marya arched her back and stretched. He imagined she was feeling as stiff as he was. She yawned dramatically and made to stand up.

"So, we are back to Princess, are we?" she asked. He could not tell if she was teasing him or if there was disappointment in her voice.

"Good morning, Marya," he said again, lacing his words with a hint of seduction.

A slow smile spread over her face.

"Good Morning, Ferrand," she replied. He liked the sound of his name on her lips. He remembered her groaning it into his mouth the previous night, and he felt himself growing aroused again. Not now. They didn't have time. They needed to get back to the ship before the crew took them for lost.

It seemed Marya agreed, as she was already shimmying into her damp undergarments. She winced as the cold, wet fabric touched her skin.

"I'm sorry we do not have time to let our things properly dry before we return," he said.

"I'm sorry we do not have more time to repeat last night," she replied, startling a laugh out of him.

"When we are married-" he stood and walked up behind her, wrapping himself around her half-dressed frame, "we can repeat it every night for as long as we both live."

Marya turned around. Her damp bloomers dragged across his groin, chasing away the growing erection with their coldness. She gave him a quick kiss on the lips. "How are we going to go back to keeping our hands off each other when we return to the company of others?" she asked.

"Well, we have approximately three more days on the ship. And, while we probably should not immediately move all your belongings into my cabin, the only other people on the ship are a bunch of sailors. It certainly will not scandalize them if we're seen holding hands as we stroll down the deck of the ship, or if I were to pull you into my arms for some kisses." He demonstrated by pressing his lips to her neck and breathing in her sweet scent.

"The servants, though," Marya replied. "Servants talk. It is sure to get around when we arrive at your castle."

"We will just have to be discreet then. Unless, of course, you want to go back to how things were between us." He silently begged her to disagree with that idea.

"I suppose a little hand-holding would not hurt anyone." She took his hand in hers and beamed up at him with a radiant smile.

They quickly dressed, and Ferrand flew them back to his ship. Fortunately, the crew had kept the ship safe through the storm, but they *had* worried about them. Ferrand was unsure what all the fuss was about when his crew had known he would go to the island. They had discussed it when Jacobe alerted him they were close. He apologized for worrying them, but he hadn't known there would be a storm.

Yet again, he had been so distracted by his personal problems with the princess that he had missed the warning signs. While he had enjoyed the results of being stranded on the island with Marya, he was disappointed in himself for missing out on the detail. He had been so eager to give the gift of freedom on the island to his future bride that he had not been cautious. He should have been on the ship to help make sure everyone weathered the storm, and he should not have put Marya in danger like that. The crew had kept everyone safe, but he would have to be more cautious in the future.

As Marya had predicted, her maid, Ellie, was the most worried. Ferrand stifled laughter when the older woman chewed her out for leaving her so worried. "Your mother hired me to take care of you, and I promised her I would do more for you than just dress you and style your hair. What would your poor mother think knowing I let you fly off alone to a deserted island with a *man* in the middle of a storm?"

Marya had held her own, though, assuring the maid it was not a big deal. Obviously, they had not known a storm was brewing. True, it was probably not proper for them to have been alone for so long. But they would marry soon anyway, and she promised to be on her best behavior until the wedding—much to Ferrand's chagrin.

Ferrand wondered if this Ellie had noticed the way Marya's porcelain skin flushed slightly at the mention of their time alone. Or the twinkle of a smile that played around her lips. If she did, she kept it to herself, and Ferrand was thankful for that. If Marya suspected that the maid was wondering about them, she would most likely pull away from him. Now that he had had a taste of her, he did not want to give it up.

XIII

Marya

On the last night before they were scheduled to arrive in Southshore, Marya and Ferrand sat together playing a game of cards. They'd come here often since returning from their island adventure, and she'd begun to refer to the combination pub-gaming hall-ballroom as the parlor.

For the last three days, Marya had been overjoyed by the renewed ease she and Ferrand seemed to feel around each other. Of course, at night, when she lay awake in her bunk, she had trouble putting thoughts of their night together out of her head. She'd be sure to suggest a brief engagement when the time came. During the day, however, they'd settled into a natural rhythm, spending most of the time enjoying each other's company and getting to know one another—well, he was getting to know her. He hadn't shared much about himself.

Marya had had little experience with card games, which were more of a man's activity in her kingdom. But Ferrand, it seemed, did not care for the nonsense of reserving specific activities for specific genders, bolstering Marya's confidence in her choice of her future husband. Of anyone she could've chosen, not only did he make the best political match, but he actually seemed to value her opinions.

Marya laid down her hand. She had a complete High Aerie—The Eagle King, his brothers the Raven and the Hawk, plus the Owl Queen and their daughter the Goose Princess.

Ferrand groaned. "I cannot believe you beat me again," he complained, setting down his cards to reveal no more than a pair of Larks and a pair of Peacocks.

"It's easy when your every expression shows how valuable your cards are. When you are disappointed, I needn't take a big risk to get a better hand," she replied.

"Am I that easy to read?" he asked.

Marya nodded. "And when you are pleased, there's no reason to play it safe. I have nothing to lose. I just plan accordingly," she continued. "Though, there is also a fair amount of luck involved. We have no control over the cards we get."

"When we are husband and wife, I will teach you a version of the game, where losing is not so bad." Ferrand winked at her. "We will have to play it in private because it involves removing articles of clothing every time you lose a hand."

Marya felt her face heating. Ever since their night in the cave, Ferrand had made comments hinting at the ways they would enjoy each other after the wedding. Marya didn't know how they'd wait that long. She yearned to feel his hands, his lips—

Ferrand was watching her closely, his eyes dark with lust. Not for the first time, she wondered if he could read her thoughts.

"Shall we enjoy the sunset before dinner?" Ferrand asked, changing the subject. "I always watch the sunset on my last night at sea in an attempt to keep it in my memory until my next trip. Sunsets on land are never quite as spectacular." How did he ignore his lust so easily?

Marya nodded and followed her betrothed to the weather deck on the ship's stern. They held hands as they walked, and a few of the sailors winked at them as they passed. Marya was sure that everyone knew what they'd been up to. Being alone together overnight in the storm, combined with their sudden change in affection for each other, it had to be noticeable. Marya tried not to let it bother her, but it surprised her to find how much her parents' views on propriety affected her. She'd miss roaming the ship hand in hand with her prince when they arrived in Southshore, but she would be glad to get away from the knowing looks.

Marya and Ferrand stood on the deck, staring out at the horizon. The sun sank lower and lower, streaking the sky with brilliant golds and oranges. The striking colors reflected on the dark sea below, making it appear as if they sailed on a sea of gold. She wished she was a painter, like her sister Olga. It was a sunset that begged to be captured on a canvas for all to admire for eternity.

Marya looked at her prince, gazing at the sight before them, and warmth spread through her chest. No matter what happened the next day in the kingdom of Southshore, once she wed Prince Ferrand, they would return to this. He had promised her a trip after the wedding. And she would hold him to it.

Though she couldn't help but wonder about what their relationship would be like. They'd shared an intimate night, but still, they hardly knew each other. Who was this man she was going to marry? He'd finally stopped pushing her away physically, but he still hadn't shared much with her emotionally.

"Tell me about your family," she interrupted the silence.

"What do you want to know?" he asked. She couldn't help but notice the lack of emotion in his voice. He was still so closed off.

"I'm not sure. A bit of everything? I am to be a part of your family soon. I should probably know more about them."

"They are not terribly interesting," he said. "My mother was human. My father is a demi-fae. His father was a full-blooded fae. He died when my father very young."

"That must have been hard for your father, raised by a human mother, with no fae influence in his life."

"I don't know much about my father's childhood. It was a very long time ago, and he never really shared much about it with me. For human families, two generations are nothing, but for demi-fae? While we are not immortal, we have long lifespans. Many wait until later in life to settle down and start a family. Many years had passed since that time in my father's life before he sired me."

"When you say 'long,' how long do you mean? Twenty extra years? Fifty? One hundred?"

"Well, not enough time has passed since the Fae Gates closed for the demi-fae in this realm to be sure exactly how long they will live," he replied. "The King of Ermaine is the oldest living demi-fae to my knowledge. He is three hundred sixty-something, and he seems to be nearing the end of his lifetime."

Three hundred sixty? Marya had known fae had long lifespans, but three hundred years was a *very* long time. And he was only a demi-fae! How old did the fae live to be?

"And other demi-fae? How old are they?" She wanted to ask him specifically how old he was, but it seemed impolite.

"In my family," Ferrand continued, "my fae grandfather lived to be three hundred fifty, but he died in the war, not a natural death. My father is one hundred fifty-two right now. There is speculation that each generation removed from our fae ancestors will live a shorter life-span. When the Gates to the fae realm were sealed, few fae remained in the human realm. They are all still living, leaving us uncertain of their lifespans. On this continent, I only know of a few demi-fae and one remaining full-blooded fae male."

"The King of Wendyl," she interrupted. She knew the major political leaders of the realm, just like any other royalty would. "And how old is he?" She wished she'd listened more to her brother and his fascination with the fae. It would've made it easier to know what she was getting into.

"Yes. The King of Wendyl. I am not sure how old he is. I have had only a few interactions with him. He fought in the fae war with my grandfather, though."

"If there are so few of your kind left, I am surprised that you do not spend more time together."

"King Nasir is a bitter man, angry that he is apart from his kin. He is not pleasant to be around. I don't envy the humans of his kingdom. He is a harsh ruler."

Marya had heard similar stories about the King of Wendyl. It was probably good she'd found a match in Southshore. She would not have wanted to live in Wendyl, where the humans were so looked down upon by their king.

"What of the other demi-fae?" she asked.

"I do not know who remains on the other continents, but I only know of five demi-fae in Torraellium—all men, except for one. You will meet my father, and my brother soon enough, and then you will know more than half of the remaining fae on our continent." Marya thought about that, wondering what it must be like to have so few of your kind around.

"It must be lonely—being one of only five demi-fae. Do you wish for the Gates to reopen so you can return to the fae lands?"

"I think my father did once. His father had planned to return, and I think my father wanted to see it. Maybe he still does."

"But not you?"

"I have more ties to the human world than I ever did to the fae realm. It was closed before I was born."

"I see. And how old are you, anyway?" She finally asked, no longer able to contain her curiosity.

Ferrand chuckled. "I am ninety-seven."

Ninety-seven? Her prince only looked a bit older than Ivan. What was it like to live for almost a hundred years? No wonder Ferrand had no concerns about taking over his father's throne soon. And poor Ivan was only twenty-two and taking on their father's crown.

"Well, you look good for your age," she joked.

Ferrand chuckled. "Do I?" he lowered his voice to a husky whisper, raising his eyebrows in an invitation, a smirk gracing his lips.

Marya's face heated. She knew that she was turning red. She wanted to encourage him, to let him send her back to the magical place they had visited on their night in the cave but knew it was not the time. His crew was all around, and who knew where Ellie might be, ready to scold her for impropriety.

"What of their human wives?" she asked, changing the subject before she gave in to her wicked temptations. "It must be tough to get old when your husband stays young and handsome."

She had meant it to be flirtatious, looking him over appreciatively from his chiseled abs upward. But when her gaze reached his face, it was obvious that it'd been the wrong thing to say. Panic flooded Ferrand's face. His eyes darted around anxiously, and he looked like he'd be sick. Had he never considered that her youth would fade long before his? She hoped she hadn't just ruined something between them.

Ferrand's voice was a low monotone when he finally responded. He did not look at her, and he spoke through clenched teeth. "I cannot speak for my grandfather and grandmother, but my parents seemed happy—even, as my mother got older. She was about your age when they married. I was born a few years later. She died in her seventies. It devastated my father. With an heir already, he had no obligations to remarry. Only a few years later, he met my step-mother, Lila. It was a shock to me when he married her, as he had seemed so heartbroken when my mother died. He is much less open about his emotions towards her than he was with my mother. Though, my Queen Lila does not seem the type to stay with a man she is unhappy with. There must be something there."

"Well, if all demi-fae are such attentive lovers—" Marya tried to lighten the mood.

Ferrand covered his ears in mock horror. "I prefer not to think of my father's skills as a lover, thank you."

Marya laughed. She had successfully eased the tension in Ferrand's features, but he had given her much to think on. Marya was quiet for a while, staring out at the horizon. The golden streaks had faded to a deep purple-blue, and only a tiny sliver of the sun remained visible.

Contemplating all that Ferrand had explained, Marya wished again that she had listened to Ivan's lectures on the fae. When she'd agreed to marry Prince Ferrand, she had not considered what it would mean to be married to a demi-fae. She had been too busy being angry that she had to marry at all. The implications of Ferrand's heritage had been the least of her concerns at the time. Why did these long-lived men put themselves through the torture of watching their wives age and eventually die?

She supposed they didn't have much choice. With so few of their kind left, it would be the only option. She thought about the lone female demi-fae. Were all the men fighting for her? Ferrand didn't seem interested, but would he have a better life if he settled with someone more like himself?

Marya wanted to know more about the fae but felt they should get back to happier topics.

"So, you have wings," she said. "What other sorts of magic powers can I expect to encounter now that I am entangling myself with a demi-fae?"

"I have wings. I have some connection with the air currents around me. I can feel when they are changing. That is why the storm came as a shock to me. I must have been *distracted*."

The way he emphasized the word distracted sent chills down Marya's spine. She had been the distraction. That she had any sort of sway over this man who seemed so strong and powerful was intoxicating.

"And you have met Geri, my familiar," he continued.

As if his words had summoned her, Geri, the falcon swooped down from her perch up near the sails and landed on the ship's deck next to them. Marya had noticed she was a large falcon the first time she saw her, but at a distance, she hadn't realized just how big she was. Standing next to her, the falcon came almost to her hips.

Marya noticed now that her wings bore a very similar pattern to Ferrand's wings.

Geri stood there, looking at her like she was waiting for something.

The bird hopped closer to her, stretching her head towards Marya, the way she had seen cats do when they wanted a scratch. Tentatively, Marya reached forward and scratched the bird on the top of the head. Geri closed her eyes. Her beak parted in what looked almost like a smile.

"She likes you," Ferrand commented. "Though, I'm not surprised. You are very *likable*."

He needed to stop emphasizing his speech that way. She knew he was talking about more than just her charming personality, and it sent jolts of heat straight to her core. She'd miss this time, only the two of them, when they arrived in Southshore. She knew it wouldn't be long until the wedding day, but it would feel like an eternity without being able to touch him. Maybe they could enjoy a little more physical contact during their last night.

"You are pretty *likable* yourself," she purred, stepping away from Geri and approaching Ferrand. She had very little experience enticing men, and she didn't know if she sounded as seductive as she meant to. When Ferrand's eyes darkened, she knew it was working.

"Oh?" he questioned.

Marya reached up and ran her fingers along the side of his jaw. "It is our last night, practically alone together. Would you like to find someplace more private where you can remind me just how much I *like* you?" She felt silly talking to him this way, but she could tell he enjoyed it.

He gripped her wrist, bringing it up to his mouth and placed a chaste kiss on her hand. The piercing gaze he gave her as he kissed each individual knuckle, and then her wrist made it feel like whatever the opposite of chaste was.

"I would like that very much," he practically growled.

Geri took the hint and soared up into the rigging somewhere to leave them alone.

"Are you sure?" Ferrand asked, concern creeping onto his face.

"What's the worst that can happen? We cause a scandal, and they force us to get married?" She laughed, trying to sound more confident than she felt.

"Can you handle skipping out on dinner?" he asked. "If you have your maid dress you for dinner, she won't question where you are if you come to my room instead."

Marya nodded. It surprised her to find that sneaking off to meet her lover had an added appeal she hadn't anticipated. Heat pooled in her belly at the thought of shunning propriety. Being the first-born child, Marya had never done anything to break the rules in her entire life. It was exciting.

Ferrand gave her one last kiss on the wrist.

Marya hurried off to her cabin to change for dinner. Her heart raced with the anticipation of what was to come. She prayed that Ellie wouldn't see how she was trembling as she replayed their night in the cave.

XIV

Ferrand

When Ferrand returned to his room, he told Leblanc he would not be going to dinner, and that he could have the night off. He knew Leblanc wasn't stupid, but it made him feel better, attempting to protect Marya's dignity. He also trusted Leblanc to keep his mouth shut. Ferrand paced his room anxiously. He had never felt this nervous about a woman before—not that he'd let himself have many. He shouldn't need to be worried. Marya would be his bride soon, as quickly as they could arrange it. The quicker, the better. Then they could get away from his father's palace and just be together.

Ferrand jumped when he heard the light rapping on his door. He opened the door to see Marya looking up and down the hallways nervously. He pulled her in quickly to save her from worry. He'd not meant to pull so hard, and she practically fell into his arms. He already scented her arousal. Before he could stop himself, he was kissing her. He pressed her up against the door as he closed it and kissed hard. She opened to him, immediately kissing him back with fervor.

"Oh, Marya," he whispered, breaking away to kiss her on her cheeks, her mouth, her neck. "I have thought of nothing else but getting my hands and lips back on you."

Marya's face was flushed, her pretty hairdo already askew.

"Slow down, slow down," she giggled as he nipped her shoulder. "If this is our last chance to be together for a while, I want to take our time. At least a little bit of time. We probably do not want to take too long. Ellie will be—"

Ferrand cut her off with another kiss. She was right, though. He should be savoring this. They might not have another chance for months. Her lips were warm and soft against his. He slid his hands along the side of her face, tangling them into her hair. A few hairpins dropped to the floor, their sound bringing Ferrand back to himself.

"I'm sorry," he said. "I just—your so—" He growled and pulled her close again.

Marya gasped, and her scent grew stronger. Skies, he had the sudden desire to ravish her right there against the door. Ferrand forced himself to break his grip on her. He had to calm himself. She wasn't stopping him, but she was also inexperienced. He needed to let her lead.

"Can—can we sit down?" Marya asked, her breathing ragged.

Ferrand looked around his room. It was larger than the other cabins, but it still contained only had a few pieces of furniture. There was his bed, a small table next to it, a writing table, a chair, and a screen with a bathing tub behind it. What would it be like to soak in a hot bath with her? There was no time to prepare it now, but when they were married—

Marya made her way towards his bed and sat on the edge. She worried her hands together in her lap. How could he ease her nerves? If he'd been feeling anxious, how must she be feeling?

"So," Marya said. Her cheeks were stained with color. She blushed so easily. He needed to make her comfortable.

Ferrand had an idea. He rummaged through the drawer in his bedside table, pulling out a deck of cards, he asked, "Do you want to play another game?"

"Will you teach me the version you mentioned earlier?" she asked. Her words were flirtatious, but she was peering at her lap, and biting that damned lip again.

"Of course," he replied. Sitting at the top of the bed, Ferrand curled one leg under himself and leaned against the headboard. He shuffled the cards and dealt them onto the bed. Marya turned towards him, crossing her legs under herself and picked up her hand of cards.

"Alright, same game we've been playing, only this time, whoever loses the hand removes an item of clothing." Marya had been able to figure out his tells quickly. He'd need to study her harder if he was going to get any of her clothing off.

Ferrand looked at his cards. Two peacocks, a lark, the Raven Prince, and the Eagle King. There were only two of each of the High Avians in the deck and six of each of the Lower Aviary birds. Should he take the safer bet and trade in his king and prince or the riskier move to try for a Full Aerie? Across from him, Marya studied her cards. He searched her face for any hint of what she was thinking. It was her move first. She discarded only one card, replacing it from the deck. Did that mean she had a good hand? If she already had most of the Aerie, there would not be many left for him. He would be better off going for the Lower Aviary.

He placed the King and the Prince in the discards, picking up another lark and another peacock. A pair and a hand of three was a mid-level hand. He kept his face neutral—at least he hoped he did.

Marya was chewing on her lip again. Ferrand wanted to suck it into his own mouth to nibble. It was a nervous habit, but was it also a tell about her cards somehow? Marya put down a single card again. She did not show even a flicker of reaction to her new card.

Ferrand could put down his larks and try for all peacocks. No. His hand was good enough. There were still so many lower birds in the deck. Ferrand set down his cards face up. Marya sighed before setting hers down as well—three larks and two peacocks. Larks and peacocks were equal. They had the same hand.

"What happens in a draw?" Marya asked.

If her face had been neutral during the game, her annoyance at the tie was clear as day. It seemed that his princess was competitive.

"It's your call," he replied. "Do we both keep our clothes on, or both remove something?"

Without answering, she looked him straight in the eyes and pulled on the ribbon, lacing the front of her gown closed. She shrugged it off without ever breaking eye contact. She sat in front of him in nothing but her thin chemise, a corset, and bloomers. Ferrand bit back a growl, his eyes roving over her body. The chemise was cut low enough that he could see the swell of her breasts thrust forward over her corset, the dark circles of her nipples visible through the thin cotton. He licked his lips.

"Alright, go on," she spoke. "Take something off."

Ferrand reached down and unlaced one boot, slowly sliding it off and leaving his leg outstretched on the bed in front of him. "You deal the next hand," Ferrand said, gathering the cards together and handing them to her.

"You cheated," she whined.

"How did I cheat?" he asked.

"One boot isn't enough."

"Why not?" Ferrand smirked at her.

"I just took off my whole dress!" she snapped.

"I never said you needed to do that."

She glared at him. "Take off your shirt, at least."

Ferrand chuckled. Skies, she was gorgeous when she was angry. "Fine. I'm implementing a new rule," he said.

Marya stared at him.

"If one player wishes the other player to remove an extra item of clothing, the first player needs to do the removing." He raised a brow at her. Would she take his bait?

"Fine." Marya set down the cards next to her and crawled towards him on the bed. She kneeled in front of him.

Ferrand held his breath as Marya slowly pulled his shirt up. When she reached the point where it came over his head, she raised herself up on her knees, bringing her body up against his. Ferrand ran his hands around her waist and cupped her bottom, pulling her tighter against him. When she did not object, he shimmied his hips and lifted her so that she straddled him. His erection pressed into her, and she ground her hips against him slightly. He groaned, the sound seemingly encouraging her. Suddenly, her hands were delving into his hair. She ripped out the leather tie, tangling her fingers in his curls.

Ferrand captured her mouth with his own, sucking that lip that'd been torturing him, into his mouth and nipping lightly. Taking her gasp as an opportunity, he plunged his tongue into her mouth. Then she did something he hadn't expected. She sucked on it—actually sucked on it. A rush of heat went straight to his groin at the thought of her sucking his cock the same way.

Ferrand tore his lips away from hers, lavishing kisses along her jawline, to her neck and up to her ear. He flicked his tongue out to taste her earlobe, eliciting a hiss from her.

"Was that alright?" he asked.

"Yes, Gods, yes," she whimpered.

He did it again, her breath hitched. So, she liked that? Ferrand sucked her earlobe between his lips and preened at the moan that escaped her lips. He snaked one hand back around to her front, sliding it up her corset and palming her breast. Marya arched her back into his touch while he gently tugged on her ear with his teeth, licking and biting his way up until he reached the rounded top of her ear.

Ferrand pulled away.

"What?" Marya asked when he stopped kissing her altogether.

"Nothing," he replied, pulling her in for another kiss. He pressed his lips against hers, and it felt amazing, but he couldn't stop thinking about her ear—her rounded *human* ear.

What of their human wives? It must be tough to get old when your husband stays young and handsome, her earlier words echoed through his mind.

XV

Marya

Something had changed. What it was, Marya couldn't identify. But Ferrand's lips pressed against hers with less enthusiasm. His hand rested lightly on her breast without any pressure or squeezing. He was pulling away from her again. Would he ask her to leave? Why did he keep doing this?

Marya ground her hips against his again, hoping for another groan like she'd caused before. He was still hard against her, but he didn't groan. *Come on, Ferrand. Tell me what I am doing wrong!* Marya tore her lips away from his.

"Alright. This is it. What have I done wrong?"

Ferrand blinked up at her, confusion evident in his eyes, "What have you—" his voice trailed off.

"I must be doing something wrong," she spat. "First, I thought you didn't find me attractive, but it's pretty obvious you do." She pressed herself into his erection for emphasis. When she got no reaction, she sat back down on the bed in front of him.

"Then, I thought you were trying to protect me," she continued. "Since I had made it clear, I only wanted a political marriage. Then I explained that was no longer the case, and I thought you agreed. So what is it, Ferrand? What keeps causing you to pull away from me? Am I doing something wrong?"

"No! Of course not." He took her hands in his. "You are not doing anything wrong. Skies above, you are doing everything right. Too right. You are so damned perfect it hurts."

What did that mean? He couldn't be with her because she was too perfect.

"No. You don't get to do that. You don't get to try to placate me by complimenting me and calling me perfect!" she yelled. "You need to tell me what is going through that gorgeous head of yours. I can't live like this—never knowing what I'm doing wrong. One minute you're kissing me and touching me, and the next, you are as cold as ice. I don't get it. If it's not something I am doing, or even if it is, tell me, please." She hated that her voice broke. She'd never begged like this in her life. She demanded things. She didn't whimper and plead.

"I'm sorry," Ferrand whispered. "I got spooked."

Spooked? By what? Was he having second thoughts about the marriage? She had given him so many chances to say it wasn't what he wanted.

"You got spooked? Are you one of those men who's afraid of commitment? Am I ruining your travel plans? Is there a different girl in each port that you're going to miss?"

"What? No!" Marya could see the hurt in his eyes at her accusation, but she was tired of this back and forth. He either wanted her, or he didn't.

"Are you afraid to settle down with just one woman? In thirty, forty years, I'll be gone, and you can go back to your solo adventures. Maybe you can find some other woman. Whatever suits you."

Ferrand pushed her away. Not hard enough to hurt, just enough to make it clear he needed space. He jumped off the bed and started pacing. Damn it. She'd gone too far. His whole body was rigid, and he wouldn't look at her.

"Ferrand?" she tried.

"You're right," he said. His voice was hardly more than a whisper. "In thirty or forty years, you will be gone, and—and I will still be here. Alone. Thinking about you every day. Missing the piece of my heart that I gave to you. Seeing your beautiful face in our children's faces. Wishing every damned day until I die that we could have had more time together." Ferrand sank to his knees next to the bed. Forehead resting against the mattress, his shoulders shook.

Marya was frozen in place. Was—was he crying? She had reduced this powerful man to tears. She hadn't known. Gods! Of course, he only wanted a political marriage with her. The alternative would be too painful. She thought about how glad she'd been that her parents left the world together so that they hadn't needed to live without the other. She'd even thought about how pleased she was that Ferrand would outlive her, but he didn't have that option. How many had he lost in his life?

"Ferrand," she whispered again, crawling towards the side of the bed where his head rested. Marya reached out and stroked his hair. He stilled. Stretching her body out on the bed, she lay on her stomach with her head next to his. She continued to run her fingers through the silky strands of his hair. The bones of her corset dug into her, and her arms ached from the angle she was reaching for him. Still, she didn't move until his breathing evened out. He pressed his head into her hand, accepting her comfort.

"Ferrand, will you please look at me?" she asked.

Ferrand turned his head to the side, looking at her, and her heart squeezed in sympathy. Hs eyes were red-rimmed, but she did not see any tears. His gaze was searching. What was he looking for?

She couldn't say the wrong thing again. Was he looking for comfort? An apology? What did he need? Marya had never been good at anything like this before. She liked things with definite answers. Emotions were too subjective.

"Ferrand, before I met you, I had no interest in marrying anyone. I wanted to be an independent woman. I wanted to be in charge of things and make my own decisions. I never saw that as a possibility as a wife. You have shown me time and again that you are going to treat me as your equal—even though, technically, we are not equal, and I'm not talking about me being female.

"We cannot pretend that you are not a demi-fae or that I am not a human. It must be awful to continuously see humans you care for die. My parents' death was the first time I experienced that loss. I cannot imagine suffering it over and over, the way you must have."

Ferrand continued to look at her, their faces only inches apart on the bed. His expression was unreadable. Marya reached out a hand, stroking his hair again. He closed his eyes, relaxing into the touch. That had to be a good sign, right?

"I don't know how you are feeling right now," Marya continued, "but I think you are the most amazing man I've ever met." And she realized, for the first time, that she meant it. "I know that I loved my parents dearly, and now that they are gone, I miss them. But I am better for having known them and loved them and been loved by them. I can only imagine you feel the same way about your mother. I want to give this thing between us a chance. But I understand, now, why you are hesitant. And if you do not want to risk an attachment to me, then please, tell me now. I will return to my room, and we can have the political marriage we originally agreed to. I will not be offended. But please, tell me what it is you want. I cannot keep guessing."

A long moment passed. Ferrand did not seem like he would reply. Her throat clogged with emotion. She wouldn't be offended if he rejected her, but she would be crushed. Rolling to the edge of the bed, Marya readied herself to leave. As she was about to stand up, Ferrand spoke. "Please," he whispered, "please stay."

Heat prickled in Marya's eyes. She let out a breath she hadn't realizes she'd been holding. "Yeah?" she asked.

Ferrand nodded. From his place on the floor, he pushed himself to standing and held a hand out to her. Marya rose, taking his outstretched hand in her own.

They stood that way for a long time before Ferrand pulled her back to the edge of the bed and sat. Marya followed suit.

Marya leaned her head on Ferrand's shoulder, and he held her closer. He kissed her lightly on the top of her head.

"You know," he murmured into her hair. "We never finished our game. I think you ought to remove that corset. If the bones are digging into me, it must be terribly uncomfortable for you."

Marya looked up at his face. He was smirking at her.

"I seem to recall," she began, "a change of rules that stated, 'if one player wished the other to remove an extra article, he would have to do the removing.'"

"Hmm, that does sound vaguely familiar," he replied. His gaze was intense, darkening to the stormy shade of blue that she was becoming well acquainted with—the one that set her insides on fire. With apparently little effort, Ferrand lifted her and laid her down on her back with her head resting on the pillows.

Ferrand nudged her bloomer-clad legs apart with his muscular thighs and settled on his knees above her. Marya was thankful she'd convinced Ellie to let her wear a front lacing corset. Ferrand tugged on the end of the bow, pulling until it came undone. Like a coil, Marya felt the garment pop open, her breasts springing loose, and her ribcage expanding. After the initial release of tension, Ferrand undid the laces the rest of the way at an achingly slow speed.

When he pulled the leather string completely free, he began a leisurely exploration of her torso. The tips of his fingers grazed her hips just below the bottom of her corset, then crept up, under the thick fabric and hard boning, over the gauzy cotton of her chemise. Up. Up. His hands glided, leaving trails of fire in their wake. Marya arched into his touch, pressing her breasts into his palms as he freed her from the last of the corset.

He thumbed her nipples, which were already erect, through the thin fabric, and a low moan escaped her lips at the sensation. Ferrand growled and met her mouth in a fiery kiss. Marya reached her arms around his muscular form, digging her fingers into his back. Ferrand slid a hand under her neck to cup the back of her head, deepening their kiss. She trailed her fingers lightly down his back and grinned as a shiver ran through him.

Ferrand pulled her to a seated position and divested her of her chemise before licking and kissing his way from her mouth to her neck, and then lower, sucking her breast into his mouth. The light scrape of teeth against her sensitive nipple sent shockwaves through her body. Marya groaned, and Ferrand dragged his teeth down the side of one breast then across to repeat the process on the other.

His hands, Marya realized, had made their way down the plane of her stomach and were untying the waistband of her bloomers. Marya lifted her hips to assist him in removing the last of her clothing, before reaching up to work on his trousers.

In the cave, Marya had not gotten a good look at his naked body. When he removed his pants, she was breathless at the sight of him. The deep cut in his muscles jutted downward as if directing her eyes to the main event. Marya swallowed hard, a rush of heat flooding her core at the sight of him. She knew where he was supposed to fit, but it was hard to believe that there would be room. Her approval must have been noted because Ferrand preened under her gaze. He flexed his muscles slightly, and Marya swallowed hard at the image of the powerful man before her.

She ached to run her hands over the firmness of his thighs, his chest, his arms, and shoulders. To feel his strength under her fingertips. Before she had a chance to look her fill, Ferrand was on her again, kissing her, licking her, stroking up and down her torso, her legs, closer, and closer to her sex. Goosebumps erupted over her skin, yet she also felt she might burn up.

She reached up to feel his muscled chest. Ferrand threw his head back and groaned at her touch. His erection was pressing into her thigh, and she knew she would only have to shift her hips slightly to let him enter her. Her insides burned in anticipation. They had said they'd wait until their wedding night, but she was starting to wonder why. Because of some arbitrary rule? Why would no one bat an eye at the idea that Ferrand had been with a woman before, but if she made love to the man she was going to marry, she'd be ruined?

Marya knew that Ferrand was the man she wanted to spend the rest of her life with. She might even be falling in love with him. Why shouldn't she share herself completely with him? Before she could come up with an answer, his exploring hands had reached the heat of her desire, and her thoughts became muddled. Ferrand plunged a finger inside of her, and she moaned again in pleasure.

After their night in the cave, Marya knew what to expect from his ministrations. As she rocked her hips into his hand, she became determined that this time, she'd see to his pleasure as well. She was not exactly sure what to do, but she imagined touching him was a logical place to start.

Marya ran a hand from his shoulder down his hard abdomen, hesitating only momentarily before finishing her decent. She wrapped her hand lightly around his erection, and he thrust his hips into her palm. The guttural noise in his throat spurred her to continue. Lightly she ran her hand to the base of his shaft and then back to the tip. This time he growled.

Marya continued to experiment with different amounts of pressure, gauging his reaction, and repeating what he seemed to like best. She was so distracted by her exploration that she didn't realize how close she was to her own climax. The tingling pressure in her core began to build, and suddenly Marya knew what was about to happen. She bit down on her cry as the pleasure crashed over her in waves. Ferrand captured her lips again with his own while continuing to coax her climax out of her.

When her body relaxed enough for her to think straight, she resumed stroking Ferrand. He was panting and grunting in her ear, and each little noise had Marya's skin prickling anew with desire. He was the most incredible being she had ever met, and she had this power over him, power to leave him gasping and panting with desire. It was intoxicating.

"Ferrand," she begged. "Ferrand, please."

"Mmm," he groaned.

"Ferrand, I want—I want to feel you inside me."

His answering growl sent a new wave of heat through her.

"Please."

"Are you sure?"

"Gods, yes. Please, I'm sure."

Ferrand shifted his hips, positioning himself at her entrance, then lingered. When he didn't enter her, she thrust her hips toward him. She felt the tip breach her sex, driving her mad, yet still, he waited.

"Please," she begged.

With frustrating slowness, he pushed himself inside her. She'd wondered how he would fit, but her body stretched to accommodate him. The fullness hurt somewhat, and she was relieved he did not move inside her. His features appeared strained, and every muscle of his body was taut.

His head dipped to her ear, and he began running his tongue over her lobe. Marya had never imagined she'd love the feel of Ferrand's hot mouth at her ear, but she was quickly learning she loved most things Ferrand did. He kept still as he licked and nibbled, rekindling the flames of her desire, and flooding her sex with heat until the pain was forgotten. As she adjusted to him, her body longed for him to move. She rocked her hips against him, burying his shaft deeper, and saw stars.

Ferrand must have taken the hint because he pulled back slowly before rocking back into her. Again, and again, he thrust into her while his hands roved over her body. Marya couldn't stop the low noises bubbling up from her throat as he lightly pinched her nipples and thrust into her repeatedly. When his other hand reached down to the place where they joined, and began stroking circles around the sensitive bud of nerves, her climax began to build rapidly.

Marya reached around to his backside, gripping his firm buttocks and pulling him tighter into her. Ferrand groaned and nipped her earlobe, again. His breathing was ragged in her ear, and his body grew taut. With a few more thrusts, he was growling her name. The rumbled sound was her undoing. Her climax crashed over her, and she met his erratic thrusts with her own gasping and panting until he pumped the last of his orgasm into her.

Marya let herself relax into the pillow, gazing up into Ferrand's eyes. They were dark and stormy but also lit with a warm glow she had not seen before. She couldn't be sure, but she thought he must see the same emotion mirrored in her own eyes. It warmed her from her head to her toes, leaving her speechless with wonder. For she was almost certain, the emotion that flickered in his gaze was love.

XVI

Ferrand

The next morning, Ferrand woke up feeling lighter than he had in ages. He hadn't realized how good it would feel to talk things out with Marya—the amazing night they shared probably wasn't hurting his mood either. Ferrand had been with a few women in his life, but it had never been like that. It terrified him, realizing that he was falling in love with Marya. But if this was what sharing a life with her would be like, he wanted to experience it—even if it meant pain somewhere in his future.

Typically, Ferrand would dread his return to the palace. His father was miserable, and they had almost nothing in common. He never knew if it would please his father or annoy him when he returned. Half the time, it had felt like his father wanted nothing to do with Ferrand, and the other half he berated Ferrand for never being around.

At least, he knew his father would be pleased with him for once. He'd sent him to win Princess Marya's favor, and Ferrand had succeeded. It was laughable to think only a week earlier he'd been so anxious and unhappy about being forced to wed. Now he could not wait for the wedding day. Especially the wedding night.

The fae, he was told, were much more open about sex. If they lived in the fae realm, no one would bat an eyelash to see the two of them together, but here in the human realm, they were to live like humans. His father saw it as the only way to keep respect. According to the king, humans outnumbered them by too much to let them have an advantage over them. Ferrand did not see how whether he and his bride were together before marriage would change that, but he knew his father would be angry if he didn't do things according to proper human customs.

Sitting in the carriage with Marya and Ellie—who had insisted on tagging along for propriety's sake—on the way to the palace, Ferrand was excited to show the kingdom to Marya. His princess seemed preoccupied. She was lost in thought, and every time Ferrand pointed something out to her, she gave a nod or a grunt of agreement and went back to her musings.

Marya twisted her hands in her lap. Ferrand reached over and placed his hand on top of hers. He earned a disapproving glare from Ellie, but the maid said nothing. Either it was not a serious enough infraction, or she saw how nervous the princess was and that he was only helping.

"What if your parents dislike me?" Marya finally blurted.

"I am sure they will like you. You are very likable," he replied. Marya flushed. He had not meant the double meaning that time, but she must have been remembering their conversation from the previous night. "Besides, my father sent me to Selmy Island with the express purpose of convincing you to marry me. Of course, he will be pleased."

"I still don't understand that. Why was your father so insistent that you marry me? What can the grand kingdom of Southshore gain from a marriage alliance with the tiny island kingdom of Selmy?"

"We've been through this. I honestly do not know," Ferrand replied. "He is probably just being selfish, wanting the alliance so no one else can have it." That would be something his father would do. Snap up an alliance just to prevent anyone else having it. Luckily for Selmy Island, they had three eligible princesses. His father could not claim them all.

They arrived at the palace, and it seemed as if most of the household had come out to greet them. His family was there, and the palace staff. Even courtiers had gathered in front of the entry. It appeared everyone wanted to greet him when he returned and possibly meet the princess. Marya's eyes were as round as the moon, and she was biting her lip again in that way that drove Ferrand crazy. Compared to her smaller kingdom, Southshore would likely take some getting used to.

Ferrand helped her down from the carriage and led her to where his father, stepmother, and half-brother were waiting.

Ferrand carefully assessed Marya's reactions to his family and his family's reactions to her. His father, who he would have expected to be pleased, looked stoic as ever. His stepmother, at least, smiled warmly. Louis just looked bored.

"Your Majesties," Marya greeted, bowing at the waist in the traditional human reception for someone of higher rank than oneself.

His father nodded his head politely.

"And who is this lovely young lady?" the queen asked.

"This would be Princess Marya Sova, eldest daughter of the ruling family of Selmy Island. And my betrothed."

"Oh, how wonderful," the queen replied. The delight in her eyes was evident. He could imagine her designing invitations in her mind already.

"Yes, an excellent match, son," the king said. "It is about time you settled down and took on some responsibilities. All your seafaring adventures have gone on long enough. A wife will be a good thing for you." Ferrand wondered why his parents were acting like his betrothal was a surprise.

The confusion was apparent on Marya's face, as well.

"Yes, Father," Ferrand replied. There would be time enough for arguing about whether or not he would be 'settling down.' It would be best not to make a scene on the palace steps with so many eyes on them.

When they completed all the required greetings to the rest of the court, Ferrand led Marya into the castle.

"I will show you to your rooms. I am sure the servants prepared a guest suite for you until the time when it is appropriate to move you to the suite of rooms next to my own. For now, I am sure you will be quite comfortable." Ferrand continued, walking and talking. Marya followed along silently. She'd been so quiet since they disembarked. A pang of worry rang through him. He hoped she didn't have sudden regrets. Now that he had let himself care for her, he did not want to lose her.

"You should rest for now," he continued as they arrived at her room. "I have much to discuss with my father. I will see you at dinner. I promise to take you on a full tour of the castle and the grounds tomorrow."

She looked like she was about to say something and then changed her mind. Ferrand kissed her on the cheek and watched her disappear behind her door.

When Ferrand arrived at the door to his father's study, the older man was waiting for him.

"All right, father, what is going on?" Ferrand asked.

"I am not sure what you mean," his father responded.

"First, you beg me to go to Selmy Island and make sure that Princess Marya chooses me as her future husband. You know I have no interest in settling down, but I agree to do it for unknown political reasons with the assurance that it is nothing more than a marriage of convenience, and I can return to my travels when all is said and done. Then, I successfully snag the princess, as you wished, and you act as if you had no idea she would come home with me, and use it as an excuse to get me to settle down and remain at home?"

"Sit down," his father commanded. "We need to talk."

Ferrand sat and stared at the king impatiently.

"I did not tell you before you left because things were still uncertain. There is a war brewing."

"A war? With whom? I thought we had reasonable alliances with all the nearby kingdoms."

"We do. Let me explain. The war will be another conflict between the fae, but this time the human's involvement will be more direct."

"How is that possible? The Gates are sealed."

"Please let me finish. The battle will not begin on our continent. I have had word, through King Nasir, that across the ocean in Dudaimash, many Dark and Light Fae still exist. They have been living in secrecy or masquerading as humans for all these years. I'm unclear why, but the King of Azria is working with the Dark Fae, who have been in hiding. They plan to unbind Deathless. If they succeed, the Dark Fae will regain their powers. There is no way it will stay contained to their lands if this happens."

"But what does this have to do with Princess Marya?" he asked.

"Selmy Island is situated directly between the Torraellium continent in the east and the continent of Dudaimash in the west. If the conflict spreads to Torraellium, it will most likely cross right through her kingdom and destroy it. King Sova has a strong naval force, but he does not have the leadership skills of his father. An alliance with Selmy will put you in a position to offer your services in leading his armada. You, a demi-fae prince, fighting for the Light side, with necessary skills to lead his fleet, married to his dear sister. You will be the perfect choice."

"What's in it for you?" Ferrand asked.

"Why does there have to be something in it for me?"

"I know you, father. You do nothing without reason. Why send your heir into battle to defend the humans?"

"This is not only about humans. The power that binds Deathless is tied to the Fae Gates. If he is free, we think the gates can open. This is both a good thing and a bad thing. When Deathless was bound, the Dark Fae lost most of their powers. We do not know how many of them there are, but between the ones who are already in this realm, and the ones who can come through the Gates, it's possible both realms will be destroyed."

Ferrand knew little about the Dark Fae. His father had glossed over that part of his education. With the Gates sealed and their leader,

Deathless, bound, there was little threat from them. It had been more important to the king to teach his son the ways of the humans among whom he would spend his life.

"If the Gates open, the remaining Light Fae will need to act quickly to destroy Deathless, lest he destroy both worlds. If we all survive this conflict, I should like to return to the Fae Realm."

"Can he even be destroyed?" Ferrand asked.

"I don't know. But we must try."

Ferrand did not think of the fae realm as home. He wanted his home to be on his ship, traveling wherever his heart took him, with Marya at his side. His father had never even lived in the fae realm. Ferrand would never understand the obsession with it.

"But you implied that I was to settle down here?"

"The war is still brewing; it might be a year or longer until any of this will become relevant. I need you to create an heir with that pretty, young bride of yours before you and I go off to war. If we do not survive, for your stepmother's and Louis's sake, we need to be sure you carry on the family line."

If Ferrand was to be running off to war, that was the last thing he wanted. He understood where his father was coming from, but it'd been unfortunate enough imagining his own life without her, someday many years down the line after decades of adventuring together. The idea of tricking her into thinking they would have the carefree life he'd promised just to get her with child and then leave them both knowing he may never return? That was awful.

"Why can't Louis carry on the line?" Ferrand asked. "And if the fae realm is open, why do we need to carry on our line here, anyway?"

"If we all survive, I would like to take Lila back to the fae realm. You and your princess can come as well. There is an ancient ritual that can be done in the fae realm to bind the life of a human and a fae together. It would shorten the fae's lifespan and lengthen the human's, so they may live together until the end of their days."

Ferrand's heart stopped. Why had he never heard of this fae magic? Was it possible that he and Marya could grow old together?

"That still does not explain why you need me to create an heir here in the human world."

"If this war reaches the same magnitude as the last fae war, you and I may not survive. If that happens, your stepmother and your bride remain here no matter the outcome of the war. Lila is not of noble birth; your mother was. The line passes through you and your future offspring. The humans will not accept Louis as their ruler. Your heir will keep this kingdom in the hands of our family—for Lila and Louis."

"I hate the way royal lineage works," Ferrand said. "If I get the princess with child, and you and I run off to die in a war, the unborn child would make a better heir than my perfectly capable younger brother?"

"It is the way it is done."

"It is stupid!".

"This war will come, whether or not you like it. I saw the way you looked at your princess when you presented her as your betrothed. If you do not lead Selmy's fleet, her kingdom will not survive this war. You may care for her, and she may care for you, but do not forget, she also married you for the political advantages. Do not let her down by letting her brother's kingdom fall."

Ferrand knew his father was right. They both got into the marriage agreement for political reasons. They would be lucky to get more than that. But the entire thing would be a waste if either of their kingdoms fell. Would it be a waste if they could be together?

For him, it would not. But he knew Princess Marya wanted to do whatever it took to save her kingdom—even something as foolish as running off to help Selmy herself. Now that he knew of the possibility to keep her forever, he would have to find a way to protect her. He could not tell her about the war just yet. He would have to wait until they had more information.

XVII

Marya

Marya was not typically one to sit around and relax, but Ferrand had left her to do just that. Not knowing her way about the palace, she decided to stay in her rooms until dinner. She had not realized how tired she was from traveling until she sat down in her room. It was strange to be back on land again. The ground seemed extra solid under her feet, and the indoor air was stale compared to the constant breeze and salty tang of the ocean air.

At first, it had felt like Ferrand was ready to rid himself of her when he left her so quickly after their arrival. But, perhaps, being an experienced traveler, he was giving her a chance to rest, knowing how exhausted she would be.

Her suite in the palace was lovely. She admired the luxurious canopied bed, swathed in filmy lace and silk in shades of cream and pastel green with pale rose bed linens. Ellie was already unpacking Marya's belongings into a large, ornately carved armoire made of a light wood unfamiliar to Marya.

"Can I hang some of your dresses in your bathing chamber, your highness?" Ellie asked. "When I draw you a hot bath, the steam will release some of the wrinkles from being packed away in trunks."

"Of course. And a bath sounds lovely when you have the chance."

The one luxury Marya had not realized how much she missed aboard the Falcon's Kiss was a proper bath. The smaller living quarters had not provided room for a full bathing tub. Marya had to make do with a washbasin and cloths. She had noticed, however, that her prince's larger cabin had a full bathtub. When they were husband and wife, she suspected travel arrangements would be much more comfortable. She felt her cheeks heating at the memory of their last night together aboard the boat. She felt the familiar itch for a run creeping in, as well.

Once Ellie had the bath ready, she helped her out of her clothing and into the tub. Marya stifled a groan as the warm water covered her. The bath was large enough that she could submerge herself to her shoulders. The heat soothed her. Marya willed her tense muscles to relax, and the itch for a run subsided. Sometimes, the way she needed to run all the time was more of a curse than a Gift. Why hadn't the Gods blessed her with something useful?

Her youngest sister Anna had one of the most sought-after Gifts in the kingdom, the ability to read someone's thoughts. Anna's Gift was relatively weak compared to the legendary soothsayers of the past, but it still seemed more practical than her own. Supposedly, there were those who could read exact thoughts from the heads of those around them as if they were their own. Anna's Gift could only give her an impression of how someone was feeling about something or a vague sense of what they wanted, and she did not use it often. She explained to Marya that she would often get a stomachache or feel physically drained when she used her Gift too much.

Marya, on the other hand, noticed nothing like that from her Gift. If anything, going for a run seemed to help her feel better, rather than worse. She loved to push herself. The night of the storm had been her last run. She would have to ask Prince Ferrand where she might do that. Would he run with her again? The warmth pooling in her core was becoming all too familiar to her.

She quickly shut off those thoughts. They had made it clear that they would follow the rules of propriety until the wedding. She hoped they could plan a short engagement. She did not know how she would stand to be around her prince without touching him or kissing him.

Marya realized the water was getting cold, and she had not even washed. She thought about summoning Ellie back for help, but she was perfectly capable of washing her hair.

After the bath, Marya returned to her bedroom. Ellie had been busy, it seemed. She had unpacked her trunks, hung her clothing in the wardrobe, and laid a fresh chemise and bloomers on the bed for her. Marya still wanted to run, but it would have to wait. She slipped into her undergarments. She was about to ring the bellpull, which she assumed led to Ellie's room, when a wave of sleepiness washed over her. A nap seemed in order. With how tired she was from their trip and comfortable the bed was, it did not take long before she was asleep.

WHEN MARYA WOKE, SHE heard Ellie poking about in her room. "Oh, good. You're awake. It's time to dress. We are back in society, and I will dress you appropriately for dinner with the king and queen of another kingdom."

Marya groaned. She had grown accustomed to her simple traveling attire. But she knew it would not be worth arguing with Ellie. She did want to make sure she made an excellent impression on the king and queen. Not only were they her betrothed's parents, but she was an ambassador for her kingdom in a way. Would they approve of her? It had been the king's idea for Ferrand to marry her. It probably did not matter what she wore to dinner—she was only a political pawn, after all. It would still feel better knowing they approved of her.

Ellie took her time styling Marya's hair in a complicated up-do, even working a copper tiara into the style. Marya tried to protest, but Ellie would have none of it. "You are a princess. You should be proud of that," she said. She dressed her in a very formal gown with heavy embroidery over a stiff corset and layers of petticoats. She hated the restrictions around her body. When she looked in the mirror, though, she could not deny that she looked like a future queen. Apart from her deep brown hair, she could have been looking at a reflection of her mother. The entire dressing routine took twice as long as Marya was used to, and it was a relief when she was on her way to the dining room at last.

Marya had not known what to expect in the palace of a demi-fae king. It was bigger and more elaborately furnished than her palace, but Marya was disappointed to find that there was very little to set it apart from any other palace. She was unsure what she had expected to find. Maybe something magical, or something strange or foreign feeling. But King Faucon's palace was as mundane as her own.

Marya was happy to sit next to Ferrand, but he barely looked at her. She nudged him under the table with her leg, and he smiled politely at her. That was it. Strange. He had seemed happy when they arrived at the palace that afternoon. What had changed since they parted?

Dinner with the king and queen turned out to be no different from banquets in her palace. The food contained the spices she had grown to enjoy during their travels, but otherwise, it was an ordinary semi-formal palace meal. Only this time, Marya felt like she was on trial. Queen Lila asked her harmless questions about her sisters and brother and giving her condolences on her parents' death, but the king, on the other hand, seemed acutely interested in what his kingdom would gain from hers. He had planned the engagement. Marya found it odd that he did not already know what advantages the alliance would afford him.

"Tell me, Princess Marya, what sort of trade deals do you think your brother would be likely to negotiate?" The king asked.

Marya hadn't the slightest idea, and she had a feeling Ivan had even fewer thoughts on the matter.

"I must admit that I have not been privy to council meetings since my brother took on the throne," she replied, hoping it would be enough to keep the king from asking too many questions. "I dare say, however, that with the rich resources of your kingdom, a match between Prince Ferrand and I is an honor for Selmy."

"Ah, yes, though I have heard many of my courtiers have developed a taste for your copper jewelry while visiting. I am sure we will come up with some trade arrangements amenable to both of our kingdoms."

She would need to write to Ivan and warn him to be careful negotiating with King Faucon.

"And what of Selmy's expectations for an alliance against outside threats?" The king continued his questioning. "Your kingdom is known for its formidable naval fleet. Is your brother prepared to come to our aid if the need should arise?"

Marya had no idea how to answer. What would Ivan want her to say? Honestly, Ivan probably didn't know himself. Negotiating an alliance with her indecisive brother in charge seemed almost as dangerous as not forming alliances. What if he let Southshore take advantage of them? A bargain on copper trading seemed reasonable enough, but Ivan knew nothing about commanding their navy. And why was this king worried about such a thing? They had been at peace with neighboring kingdoms since before Marya's lifetime.

Her father had included her in the kingdom business, but by the time Marya had started following her father around, their foreign affairs were well established. And Ivan knew even less about such matters. Meeting with King Faucon only reinforced her ideas that Ivan had no idea what he was doing.

Marya twisted her hands in her lap and fidgeted her leg. Was she making the right choice? Would marrying Ferrand even be in Selmy's best interest? If King Faucon was as greedy as Ferrand had implied, and he had more political ambition than her brother, he would not be looking out for her kingdom. He would look out only for his own.

After the previous night with Ferrand, it was tempting to say, "yes," out of pure selfishness. With Ferrand acting so odd since they had arrived, she didn't know what to think. He barely looked at her throughout the entire meal. Had she done something wrong? Was he just unhappy to be back home? She knew he had a strained relationship with her father. Hopefully, that was the cause of his sour mood and not something to do with her.

She could hardly imagine life without Ferrand now that they had agreed to try for more than just a political union. He had awoken something inside of her she had not known existed. She could not wait until they could be together as husband and wife whenever they wanted—if he even still wanted her.

She would just have to talk to him about it. They had promised no more secrets or misunderstandings between them.

THE NEXT DAY, FERRAND left Marya alone all morning. He and the king had holed up in his father's office. Considering her prince had said that he did not get involved in the business of the kingdom and didn't get along with his father, he sure was spending an awful lot of time with him. When they had said they would keep their relationship casual until the wedding, she hadn't thought it meant staying completely apart.

Marya, Queen Lila, and Louis were eating luncheon together when she saw him at last. Queen Lila had been asking about her favorite flowers when Prince Ferrand and his father appeared in the doorway to the room. They were deep in discussion, but their conversation stopped as soon as they passed the double doors. The king made his way to his place at the head of the table, stopping to press a chaste kiss on his wife's cheek. Louis sat in the seat Ferrand had occupied at dinner. Ferrand ruffled his brother's hair before taking the seat next to him.

Marya's heart gave a squeeze at the sight of the paternal gesture. What kind of father would Ferrand make? She thought about the way he had comforted her after her nightmare, or his patience while teaching her to play cards. She could feel a grin spreading on her face as he sat across from her. He smiled back at her, raising a questioning eyebrow. She shrugged her shoulder.

"You have been busy this morning, Prince Ferrand," Marya said. "I had hoped for a tour of the palace. I had to ask one of the servants how to get back to the dining room this morning."

"Yes. I am sorry about that. My father and I had some business to attend to." His voice was stiff. What was he hiding from her?

"Take your princess on a tour this afternoon," the King replied. "I shan't need you this afternoon. We will have a meeting tomorrow with King Nasir from Wendyl, however."

"Of course," Ferrand replied.

No one said much after that, and Marya found herself watching Ferrand eat—the bob of this throat when he swallowed, the movement of his mouth as he sipped the spicy soup off his spoon. Warmth pooled in her belly, and Ferrand's eyes met hers in a heated gaze.

"All right, Princess, let's take a tour," he announced, standing abruptly.

Marya jumped to her feet, her cheeks heating as he led her from the room.

"What was that?" he murmured as she placed her hand lightly in his elbow.

"What?" she asked innocently.

Ferrand chuckled, leading her down a stone hallway. He showed her where the ballroom was, and where there were some sitting rooms, and they passed the door to the king's office. It disappointed Marya, yet again, that other than the size, nothing about the castle stood out differently from her own. And Ferrand was quiet again. She could have wandered around on her own and had a more interesting tour.

They were heading down another hallway, which Ferrand had explained led to the library when a painting of the king caught her eye. "You look just like your father, you know," she commented. "You have the same eyes." She turned and gazing up at him. "Yours look happier, though."

He made a little huffing noise and rolled his eyes.

"And your smooth, bronze skin," she continued, reaching a hand up and stroking it across his cheek. He stiffened under her touch. "You know, before I met you, I imagined all the fae, especially the wind fae, as pale and wispy. Like the pictures in children's books of fairies and wind sprites, but you are certainly not wispy," she ran her hand down the column of his throat. She felt the bob of his throat as she trailed her fingertips lower to grip the firm muscles of his biceps.

Ferrand grabbed her hand and pulled it off. Why? She looked up at him, pouting. Gods. Had she just pouted at a man to get his attention?

"You know," he said, changing the subject. "We have some books in the library with images of actual fairies and wind sprites. I've heard my grandfather's collection of books in the fae realm was even more extensive, but he brought some books with him as a gift to my grandmother's family library when they were to be wed. This was her family's palace." He took her arm and leading her into the library as he talked. "Her family had no male heir, so my father took it over when he was old enough."

Marya gasped when she saw where he was leading her. This was what she had been hoping for, something that screamed "magic."

The collection of books from the Fae realm was on display in a glass case at the back of the library—three books bound in pale leather, with beautiful lettering embossed on their spines. Golden, bronze, and amethyst letters shone with their own iridescence.

The wooden book stands on which they were displayed would have been exquisite for any other book collection, but next to the fae books, they looked dull and ordinary, lacking the inexplicable luster of the books.

"Finally," Marya breathed.

"Finally, what?"

"I was thinking I had moved into the only fae palace in the lands containing nothing magical."

"I am sorry to disappoint you, but not only have very few relics from the fae world survived in this one, but my father is insistent that we live as humans do."

"Really? My sister Anna will be incredibly disappointed. I think she was expecting a magical fairy palace when she comes to visit. She's a bit of fanciful. She is insanely jealous of my marrying a 'gorgeous fairy prince.' I think that is how she referred to you."

Marya paused, waiting for a saucy quip about her calling him gorgeous. When none came, she sighed dramatically. What was he hiding from her?

"All right, Prince, Let's look at these Fae books. I should probably learn what I'm getting myself into." Ferrand winced slightly at her cold tone, but didn't say anything.

Ferrand opened the glass case and pulled out a book, with shimmering gold lettering, and placed it atop the table in front of them. They studied the book together for a while. Ivan would have loved this. The book was written in the language of the fae, so Ferrand had to translate for her.

Learning about the fae types—fire, earth, water, and wind, along with smoke, poison, and blood—was somewhat interesting, but a history lesson was not what she'd had in mind for their tour.

"We have some books about the Fae in our library back home," she commented.

"Yeah?"

"My brother, Ivan, is a bit of a fae fanatic. He studies all the information he can find about the fae. I thought he might wet himself when he found out he was getting a fae brother-in-law. Honestly, I'm surprised he did not try to marry you himself!" she teased.

Ferrand chuckled.

"I have not really read any of Ivan's books myself," she continued. "I wonder how accurate they are, with humans having written them. Can I show these books to him when he comes in for the wedding?"

"I don't see why not," he replied. "We should probably think about when we want to hold the wedding. Just wait until my stepmom gets ahold of you. She is beside herself to be planning a wedding. Don't let her bully you, though."

"So, you do still plan on marrying me then?" she asked.

"Of course."

"I wasn't so sure, since you seemed bent on ignoring me ever since we arrived in Southshore."

"I'm sorry. It's not you. My father has me preoccupied."

"With what?" She asked.

"It's nothing."

"It's obviously not nothing. You promised no more secrets between us."

"I know," he replied. "I cannot tell you about it just yet."

"But you *will* tell me?"

A lengthy pause fell between them. Marya looked at him expectantly.

"You will find out in time," was all he said. Marya crossed her arms and glared at him. Had their entire conversation in his cabin meant nothing? He had promised to include her things. Hadn't he?

XVIII

Ferrand

The next day, Ferrand and his father met with King Nasir from Wendyl. He was their only source of information on the coming war, and Ferrand was unsure of how much he trusted the information. Why did Nasir know so much about the plans of the Dark Fae? Who were his informants in Azria?

Ferrand and his father rarely agreed on anything, but they were both more concerned about protecting the human world than King Nasir was.

"Is there any way to destroy this Dark One permanently?" Ferrand asked.

"They call him 'Deathless' for a reason," King Nasir replied, running a hand through his short, wavy, blond hair. Ferrand hadn't known why they called him Deathless. He barely knew anything about this ancient leader of the Dark Fae. His father's insistence on raising him like a human was frustrating. Ferrand wondered if possibly his father pretended to be uninterested in the fae history because he also did not know much about it. Ferrand's grandfather had died when he was only a few years old, and humans had raised him.

"Besides," King Nasir added. "If the power binding him, really is tied to the Gates, destroying him could destroy the Gates. I have been here long enough, as have the fae who remain in Azria and the other Dudaimash kingdoms. We want to go home to Briphaelium."

Briphaelium? Ferrand had never even known the name of the Fae realm. If someone had asked him days ago if he cared about the destruction of the Gates or going to Briphaelium, he would have said 'no,' but now that he knew there was a chance to extend Marya's life, he did not want to lose that opportunity.

"So, we let the Dark Fae release him? And then we fight them?" Ferrand's father asked. "That seems like a risky plan. So many will lose their lives—humans and fae alike. Especially if, as you say, there is no way to destroy him."

"He grows more powerful, as he gains Dark followers, perhaps if we take out his followers, he will be weak enough to kill," King Nasir suggested.

"So why can't we seek out his followers before they can free him? You seem to have contacts among the Fae in Dudaimash. Do they know where these followers are?"

"Maybe the ones in this realm, but we have no idea how many survive in Briphaelium."

Ferrand's head was spinning. It seemed they were stuck in a cycle. There was no way to open the Gates without freeing Deathless. His followers had no power without him being unbound, but they would find a way to liberate him. He would have less power if his followers were killed, but there was no way to kill the followers without opening the gates—for which they would need to free him.

When King Nasir finally left, Ferrand felt he had no more answers than before their meeting. It was the type of thing he would love to talk to his princess about. She was so much better at political dealings than he was. First, he needed to figure out how he would protect her because as soon as she found out her kingdom was in danger, who knew what she would do?

It seemed no matter what they did, however, a war was coming. A dangerous war, that if they won, would lead to his ability to live out his days with the woman he loved. But at what risk? What were the chances they would both survive?

FERRAND HAD PROMISED to spend the afternoon with Marya, to take her on a tour of the castle grounds. Show her the gardens and the lake, and the best places to run. But with so much on his mind, he was regretting it. He would have a hard time keeping his worry from showing. He knew Marya wanted him to include her in running a kingdom. But when he had promised she could, he had not known it would involve a dangerous war.

He found her in his stepmother's favorite sitting-room pouring over a book of fabric samples.

When she looked up, her smile lit her whole face, wrapping around him like a warm embrace. He would never tire of her smile, and to think he might get to keep it for a hundred years or more. Ferrand had a feeling that his answering grin was just as big as hers. She scooted over to make room for him.

Ferrand obliged. His larger frame, and the bulk of Marya's dress, left them crowded on the small, delicate sofa. Ferrand had never felt comfortable in the overly feminine rooms his stepmother had decorated. He often forgot she was not noble born. She took to her life as queen very well.

"I am having Marya choose out fabric for a new wardrobe," Lila said when he was seated. "Her gowns are lovely but completely impractical to the heat here."

He liked the idea of Marya in the floaty gauzy dresses his stepmother and the ladies of their court preferred.

"Ellie will not be happy," Marya commented. Ferrand chuckled. For all that she seemed to worry about what Ellie would think of things, the maid did not seem to have much control over what Marya did.

"I like that green fabric," Ferrand suggested. "It matches your eyes."

Marya's face stained with color. He never realized how easily women with pale skin like Marya's blushed.

"The green will be lovely," Lila agreed.

"Honestly, I do not care," Marya commented. "As long as I can get out of these heavy dresses, I will be happy. Choose whatever you think is best."

His stepmother looked a bit disappointed. He wondered if she wished she had daughters of her own to plan dresses with.

"Are we still going for a tour of the grounds?" Marya asked.

"Let's go," he replied, jumping to his feet and offering her his arm.

Marya took his arm with a smile, and he led her out of the palace. He took her through the gardens, which she had called lovely, but did not seem overly impressed with. The palace sat in the center of a plateau at the edge of the peninsula. While Ferrand knew the ocean views on the cliffside were spectacular, he knew that they would be similar to the views from her palace grounds. Where could he take her to impress her?

"Where do you think it would be best for me to do my running?" Marya asked, interrupting his thoughts and giving him an idea.

"I know the perfect place," he said, leading her further away from the palace itself.

"At home, I went for a run every morning, often waking before anyone else," she explained as they walked. "Do you think anyone will be terribly shocked if I took up the same practice here?"

"I can't imagine anyone will be; they are used to Louis and I flying around," he replied, thinking he may have to take up running as a hobby himself. Spending so much time on his ship, Ferrand had no trouble waking up early. It seemed his father would keep him very busy during the day. Sneaking in a morning run with his princess sounded like a brilliant idea.

They passed last of the palace's outbuildings, and the enormous rolling meadow beckoned in front of them. Gently sloping, grassy hills stretched out ahead of them. In the distance, Ferrand could just make out where the grass transitioned to stone before ending abruptly at the cliffs that overlooked the ocean. He wondered if Marya could make out the cliffs with her human eyesight.

She must have liked what she could see if her gasp of excitement was any sign.

"So, Prince," she crooned. "In proper daylight and without flying, who do you think could run faster?"

"I have never seen just how fast you can run, but I still think I could outrun you."

"Do you want to race?" she asked.

Ferrand chuckled. He would rather just watch her, but he would play.

"Sure," he replied. "There is a lake if you run straight south. Let's see who can get there first."

Marya nodded. "Ready. Set. Go!" She called and took off faster than he had yet to see her run.

Ferrand watched her for a moment, her poufy dress a stiff bell around her legs, her formal hair style threatening to come free.

Ferrand realized he had better get moving if he would catch up to her. He launched himself forward, his heavy boots pounding on the grass. He had dressed for a formal meeting with a foreign king, not for a run. He supposed he still had an advantage over Marya, who was sure to have a tight corset on under her gown.

Ferrand missed a step, thinking about the last time he had seen her corset. Had that been only two nights ago? It was beginning to feel like she had always been a part of his life. Ferrand shook himself out of his thoughts and pushed forward. He had let her get too much of a head start on him. He was catching up slightly, but he could see the lake coming into focus, and she was much closer than he was.

Tendrils of her long hair were slipping loose, and Ferrand wondered how annoyed Ellie would be when she came in a windswept mess. Ferrand knew it was cheating, but he wanted to catch her. He slowed down but did not stop, stripping off his belt and tunic as he ran.

His wings burst open, and he took off, flapping heavily until he was right behind her.

He had thought to dispel his wings and run the rest of the way, but he noticed she was nearing the lake, and not slowing at all. Did she not see it? Ferrand flew towards her, grabbing her around the waist just as she was about to run headlong into the water.

Marya froze in his arms, but she must have quickly realized what was happening. Her body relaxed, and she threw her arms out to catch the surrounding wind. Ferrand flew them over the lake, setting her down on the opposite shore and dropping to stand next to her.

Her face was flushed, and her breathing was labored. Her eyes were wild with energy. Ferrand pulled her close to him in a searing kiss. She melted into his arms, and he curled his wings around her.

Marya broke the kiss first.

"You cheated," she said, just as he had known she would.

"Would you rather I let you run straight into the lake?" he asked.

Marya laughed. "No."

"I mean, I would love to come out here for a proper swim with you sometime, but I didn't think letting you run into the lake in your heavy gown was the best idea. Were you paying any attention?"

"Not really," she laughed again. "I sometimes get so lost in the feelings of the ground slipping away beneath my feet and the air whipping around me, I don't always pay enough attention. Back in Selmy, I was so familiar with the paths I usually ran that I didn't have to think. I always wound up in that clearing where Geri spied on me."

Ferrand chuckled.

"Though I will admit, I am not used to it being this dreadfully hot when I run. Is it always like this?"

"Well, it is summer now. This is the worst it gets. I imagine you will be more comfortable with the new wardrobe Lila is ordering for you."

"I hope so. The seamstress will come tomorrow to take my measurements—and plan my wedding gown. It will probably take us all afternoon." She groaned, throwing herself down on the grass.

"You don't sound pleased." He sat on the grass next to her.

"It is sure to be a dull way to spend the afternoon. What is on your schedule tomorrow? Another morning cloistered in your father's study?"

"He hasn't mentioned," Ferrand replied. He sure hoped not.

"What has had you so busy?" she asked. He was not ready to tell her about the coming war. She would want to get too involved.

"Just the usual. Kingdom business," he lied.

"Funny. I seem to remember you mentioning you liked to stay completely uninvolved in the daily kingdom business. That I would be an amazing asset to you because I would be so helpful." Her voice was sharp, and her body was tense. "So, either you lied to me then, or you're hiding something from me now."

"It's nothing. I promise." His gut clenched, and a wave of nausea rolled over him. He had promised her, no more secrets, and now he was lying to her.

Marya did not even say a word. Her hands were clenched in tight fists as she got up. She stalked towards the palace without even a backward glance. Ferrand remained where he was, staring at the water. He wanted to protect her, but not at the cost of the growing tenderness between them. Would it be worth getting to grow old with her if she was always angry at him?

XIX

Marya

Ferrand hadn't been kidding when he said his stepmother was excited to plan their wedding. Over the next few weeks, she and the Queen were so busy she didn't have much time to think about Ferrand's odd behavior. There was so much to do. She barely saw her betrothed.

Not that she would have seen him much if she wasn't busy. The king and Ferrand spent all day in meetings. The King of Wendyl had been back to visit twice. Marya couldn't imagine what they were working on. Southshore seemed to be a flourishing kingdom.

It practically ran itself. It was divided up into four counties, each run by a count. The counts made all the decisions for their counties and collected a tithe from their villages and cities, which was, in turn, paid to the king. She wondered why Selmy didn't have a system like that. Possibly it was just too small to warrant it.

She thought it could be helpful to Ivan to have people under him doing the bulk of his job. Maybe they could have just two small counties that could run themselves. Uncle Tavar would know how to run half the kingdom. They could give one county to him and the other to one of the Digbys. It would take some pressure off Ivan. He could be the final say when their policies conflicted or when dealing with foreign kingdoms, but he needn't worry about the day-to-day business of running the kingdom.

Marya tucked the idea away to suggest to him. If no one allowed her to help him directly in the kingdom's affairs, she would note how the thriving kingdom of Southshore did things and give him some ideas. She wanted to establish trade of summer fruit for winter berries.

It would mean delicious fruit all year long for both kingdoms. She wanted to see what they could do about getting the Southshore spices she was growing to love into Selmy.

Marya did not have a lot of time to contemplate trade deals, though, with Queen Lila keeping her busy all day. Planning a wedding was a much more massive undertaking than she had realized. After endless days writing invitations, choosing a menu, deciding on decor, and being fitted for her wedding gown, Marya was exhausted.

One afternoon, when she had some free time to herself, she went exploring the grounds. She had not spent a lot of time outdoors since her tour with Ferrand. Every morning she went running in the meadow before it was too hot. The flat, even grass, meant she could push herself. A few times, Ferrand had also joined her. But that was it.

With the sun shining above and an afternoon to herself, Marya visited the lake. She sat on the bank, her shoes off, her dress pulled up to her knees, and her feet dangling in the cool water. Thank Oola, fashion in Southshore did not involve wearing large puffy skirts with many layers or hoops except for formal events. Ellie did not like to leave Marya's best dresses hanging in the closet untouched, but as the weather continued to grow hotter now; she had conceded that the dresses the ladies of the Southshore court wore were more appropriate. Marya loved the gauzy floaty skirts, and lack of corset.

It was hot out all the time, and with Marya's fair complexion, if she spent too much time in the sun, her skin grew red and irritated. She wondered what she could do about it. She loved being outdoors too much to hide in the palace all day.

Marya swished her feet in the chilly water, but with the sun beating down on her from above, it did little to cool her. It was difficult to concentrate on her worries where her betrothed was concerned. When they saw each other—which was not a lot with how busy they both were—Ferrand was pleasant and affectionate, but he was obviously keeping something from her. She had asked him repeatedly about his meetings with his father, but he always shrugged it off.

He had promised to treat her as an equal. Not only was it frustrating how little she'd seen him, but what were he and his father keeping from her. Why was he spending all his time with the king he claimed to hate?

Had she done something wrong? Something to upset him? She didn't think so, but she just could not understand him. She was having trouble thinking about anything in the blistering heat, though. She would just need to forget about it. She would go back to thinking of it as a political match to help her kingdom. When Ivan came in, she would suggest all the things he should negotiate with King Faucon and forget about what Ferrand thought of her. She had never let anyone else's opinions of her matter before.

With that settled, she would have to head back to the palace soon. She would make herself sick sitting in the blistering sun for too much longer. Out by the lake, she could avoid Queen Lila and wedding planning. If only the water cooled her entire body, instead of just her legs.

Maybe she could submerge her entire body in the cool lake. She wondered if she dared. Would it ruin her dress? She didn't think so. And if it did, well, she had other dresses. Marya looked around, not seeing anyone, she slipped into the refreshing water. She knew how to swim. She and her siblings had spent some time swimming in the ocean as children, but she was no expert.

Marya didn't need to be an expert. Alternating between treading water, and floating on her back, was good enough, and the lake water felt wonderful on her hot skin. Marya was floating on her back, lightly kicking her feet to keep them afloat when she heard a loud splash. Her feet dropped instantly beneath her as she came back upright to see what had made the noise. She watched water rings rippling away from a point on the other side of the lake. Whatever it was, it was still underwater.

Marya inched back towards the edge of the lake. She was not sure she wanted to know what she now shared it with. Keeping her face towards the spot where the thing was, she felt the grassy edge of the pool against her back. She tried, but she could not lift herself out of the water without turning her back to whatever it was. She debated what to do, but before she decided, Prince Ferrand's head poked up from a spot not too far from her.

Water slicked his jet black hair down, along the sides of his face, the bulk of his ebony locks floating around his shoulders where it lay on the surface of the water. Droplets of water ran down his face and dripped off his jaw. He pushed himself further out of the water, revealing the thick column of his neck and his broad shoulders, water streaming down his smooth, bare, copper-brown skin. Marya swallowed hard, a now-familiar heat blossoming in her belly. How was he standing? He was taller than her, but not that much. It must have been shallower on that end of the lake; it made him seem immense like he would tower over her. If he summoned his wings at that moment, she would have sworn he was a god. He could have been Otreus himself, come to her from the Skies Above.

Her breath caught in her throat. Her newfound determination to forget about having more than a political arrangement wavered as she followed a droplet of water with her eyes. Thank Oola the water stopped high enough she couldn't follow it much lower than his collar bone. The darkening of his eyes and the tiniest of smirks playing around his lips told her he knew exactly what she was thinking.

He was looking at her like he might devour her, and she thought she might let him. Then, like a flash, he was gone. He dove under the water, swimming and coming up near the far bank. He flipped himself onto his back and started swimming. Long, languid strokes like windmills sent him gliding across the lake in a smooth straight line.

Thank the Gods, when his legs floated up to kick at the surface, they were still clothed. She had been wondering. He swam the entire length of the lake on his back.

When he reached the bank where she was still treading water and staring like a fool, he did some sort of flipping, spinning maneuver, and took off the way he came. This time he swam on his front. The lines of his body remained smooth, barely causing more than a ripple in the clear lake water. Marya tried not to stare, but his smooth cotton trousers clung to his body like a second skin in the water. They outlined every inch of his muscular lower half from his calves up through the backs of his thighs and over the sensuous curve of his backside.

Marya bit her lip, sucking in a deep breath, imagining his powerful legs pressed up against her body. Part of political unions involved making babies right? Just because she didn't care what he thought anymore didn't mean she would not have to give him up completely. She wasn't quite ready to be a mother, but she knew their arrangement involved making an heir, and she let herself imagine how much she would enjoy the process.

Prince Ferrand continued swimming the length of the lake. He swam back and forth for many laps. Marya chewed on her lip, wavering about whether to stay or go. On the one hand, she could continue avoiding the queen and wedding planning if she stayed. She could even join Ferrand in his laps, but next to the prince's elegant strokes, she would look like a floundering child. Or, she could go, but she knew that the moment she stepped from the water, the flowing cotton dress she was wearing would behave exactly as Ferrand's trousers had. She had planned to sit in the sun and dry herself, at least partially, before returning to the castle.

Her arms and legs were getting tired, treading water. The prince had seen her in a wet dress before. He'd seen her in less. It was not as if he was paying her any mind, anyway. He had not even looked at her since starting his laps. She reminded herself that it didn't matter. She didn't care what he thought. Not anymore. She didn't need him. She had never needed anyone, and she didn't need anyone now. She pulled herself out of the water and stalked off towards another sunny part of the property without so much as a backward glance to see if he was watching.

Marya made her way to the meadow, where she knew there would be plenty of sun. She found a soft patch of grass and tiny purple wildflowers and sat down. She spread her skirt out as wide as it would go, hoping the relatively thin fabric would dry quickly. Knowing she wouldn't go anywhere for a bit, Marya lay the rest of the way down on the grass and closed her eyes. She brought her hands to her heart and took several deep breaths. A sweet scent drifted towards her, probably from the gardens nearby. She listened to the birds chirping around her. A bumblebee buzzed somewhere nearby.

Marya did not know how long she lay in the grass. She might have been dozing, she could not be sure, but she jolted upright at the sudden feeling she was being watched.

Above, she noticed a large falcon circling in the sky. Geraldine. Had Ferrand sent her as a spy? Marya's heart thumped harder in her chest, thinking he might be watching her. Was he missing her? Was he just interested in her soaked, flimsy gown? Was he as aroused as she had been by his wet body? No matter how much she tried to put him out of her mind or pretend she didn't care, she couldn't help it. Just a few weeks ago, she had thought she was falling in love with him. Now he was a mystery.

Marya waved at the bird, to indicate she knew that she was there. Geri spiraled down in a wide circle, landing on the grass a short distance away. Marya stretched her legs out and patted the ground next to her in invitation, the way she would call a puppy. The enormous bird hopped over to her.

She had been in Southshore for nearly a month, and Marya realized this was the first time she had been alone with Geri. She had seen her in the distance a few times. And Ferrand had introduced them on the ship. However, she had never been around the falcon alone. How was she supposed to act?

She had forgotten just how big Geri was. While Marya remained sitting, the falcon's eyes were almost level with her own. The bird blinked at her a few times.

What did one say to a giant bird that could communicate telepathically with her fiancé?

"Hello, Prince Ferrand," she spoke to the bird. "If you wanted to spy on me, you need only to have followed me yourself."

The falcon tilted her head like she was listening. Marya smiled. "Can I pet you?" she asked. Geri lowered her head and stretched her neck.

"I'll take that as a yes?" Marya reached her hand towards her making slow, cautious movements. She lightly scratched the falcon on the head. Her feathers were soft. They reminded her of her prince's feathers.

"What does he want, Geri?" Marya asked. "I cannot figure him out,"

The bird rubbed her head into Mary's hand.

"I wish he would talk to me. I suppose I could talk to him. But, I've tried asking him nicely to tell me what is going on. Do I need to nag him and pester him? Everything was so easy when we were on the boat. What changed?"

Geri shrugged her wings up and down the same way humans gestured, "I don't know."

"You can understand me?"

The falcon bobbed her head up and down as if she was saying, "yes."

"Can you talk to me, the way you talk to Ferrand?"

Geri shook her head.

"But you can talk to Prince Ferrand, right?"

Geri nodded again.

Talking with a hawk was a novel experience for Marya. It would be difficult to have a conversation that comprised only "yes" or "no" questions. She guessed it was better than having no one to talk to at all.

"So, Geri, what do I do? Does Ferrand care about me? Does he think of me as an equal like I dared hope? Will he take me on grand adventures on his ship like he promised? Or was it all just empty talk to get me here for a stupid political arrangement I would have agreed to, anyway?"

She shrugged again.

It startled Marya when the enormous bird pressed herself entirely against her. At first, she thought the bird was trying to knock her over, but she nuzzled her head against Marya's abdomen, like a cat might. Marya thought she might be trying to comfort her. Then Geri further surprised her by lowering her upper body across Marya's lap. She had never cuddled a bird before, but that was clearly what the bird wanted.

She stroked Geri's feather's absently until they were both dozing in the afternoon sun.

XX

Ferrand

Ferrand could not rid of the image of Marya emerging from the lake from his head. She was a siren come to lure him to his death. The cotton dress she wore had clung to her body, showing him every curve of her womanly figure. He had needed to dunk himself back under the water to stop himself from leaping out of the lake, grabbing her by the swell of her hips, and driving himself into her.

He knew that she wanted him. There was no question, in the way her eyes traveled down his own wet body, or in the sweet scent of her arousal whenever they were alone together—which had not been as frequent as he would have liked over the past several weeks. In a way, he was thankful for his stepmother's interest in wedding planning, and for his father's war councils. The less time he saw his betrothed, the less he needed to avoid filling her in on the details of the war.

The seemingly impossible war. They debated over long hours what would be the best strategy to assist the remaining Light Fae in Dudaimash. Should they plan to help from the start? Should they wait until the battle made it to their shores? Was there a way to destroy Deathless without destroying the Gates? Or should they let the Dark Fae free him? And then fight him? No one knew how strong he and his followers were. The debates cycled on and on.

King Nasir only cared about getting himself and any other fae and demi-fae who were interested back to the fae realm—*Briphaelium*, Ferrand reminded himself. Some fae he was, not even knowing the name of their lands. King Nasir didn't care if their strategy involved sacrificing the humans who called this land their own, as long as he could return home.

They had had no support one way or the other from Ermaine. The king was old and sickly, nearing the end of his demi-fae life, or so Ferrand had been told. His son, Prince Gavril, was frivolous and immature. He had returned none of their missives to discuss the situation. From what Ferrand remembered of him from his one and only visit to southshore, Gavril was a huge flirt, and spent most of his time dallying with human courtiers, not thinking about the politics of the kingdom. Ermaine was off the table as an ally unless Prince Gavril got his act together, or his father miraculously became well again.

Ferrand's Father continued to insist that if he went to Selmy Island and took on command of their naval fleet, it would give them the best chances in the war. He loved being on the water in a ship, but not as a battle commander, as a sailor. He still didn't feel right, leaving Marya on her own. It was all so frustrating.

"Ferrand, have you seen your young lady?" A voice broke into his thoughts. It was his stepmother. She stood in front of him in the castle library. Ferrand had begun reading his father's fae books in earnest, looking for any scrap of information that could help them.

"I saw her out by the lake. But that was hours ago. I do not know where she is now."

"What do you mean you do not know?" Lila asked. She had a look of concern on her face. "Is something wrong between you two?"

"What makes you ask that?" Was something wrong?

"When you first arrived at the palace together, you looked at her with the most adoring grin. Like she was Queen Oola herself and had hung the moon for you." Ferrand did not remind his stepmother that the fae, including he and his father, did not follow the same pantheon of Gods that the humans did. Ferrand, having been raised in the human world, knew that not only was Oola the Queen of all the human Gods, but an owl represented her, just like the Sova family crest. Lila's comparison held up, and he did wish to worship Marya like a goddess.

"And?" he prompted her to continue.

"And for the past few weeks, I have noticed you spend less and less time together. What changed?"

"Nothing. We knew from the start we were making a political union, and nothing more."

"That may be, but sometimes, although we do not plan for a love match, we find one. Marya is an intelligent, beautiful young woman who will make you a wonderful queen someday."

"Will she, though?" Ferrand asked. "With this war coming, the chances of us both surviving are so low." Ferrand clamped a hand over his mouth. Had his father told Lila about the war? Skies, he would be angry if Ferrand had just revealed it to her."

"Oh, relax. I know all about the Fae war that is coming. Your father trusts me with all his business."

"He does?" Ferrand raised an eyebrow in surprise. Lila was born a commoner. And his father had never seemed as close to her as he had been to his first wife, Ferrand's mother.

"Ferrand. Do you know how I ended up with your father?"

"No. Honestly, it was a total shock to me when I came home one day, and here you were."

"You know your father loved your mother very much. When she died, it hurt him a lot."

"I know. It is one reason I was anxious not to get too close to Marya."

"Your father would be the first to tell you it was worth it."

Ferrand thought back to the days after his mother's funeral. He had been old enough to take care of himself, but his heart had ached with the fresh hole formed by the loss.

"Those years he spent with your mother were the happiest of his life, and it brought him you. He may not always show it, but he loves you so much. It is one of the reasons he hates your constant traveling. He wants you here."

"He has a funny way of showing it."

"Yes. He is not always the brightest man. Anyway, back to my story. For many years after your father lost your mother, he used to frequent the same human tavern, up in the northern part of the kingdom, where he hoped no one would recognize him as the king. He would spend weeks there drowning himself in strong drinks and pretending to be just a commoner. That tavern belonged to my father. I was only ten or eleven when he first started coming. He was always kind to me. Over time, I got older, and I would fantasize about his visits. He was, and still is, a very handsome man. I did not know who he was. I thought he was just some nobleman who liked my father's liquor.

"As I got older, I often tended the bar for my father, and one night, your father, completely intoxicated, spilled his whole life story to me. I realized that I could not let him tell anyone else who he was. It was foolish of me, but I lured him up to my room, where I had planned to let him sleep off his drink.

"When he woke the next morning, he panicked, not remembering much from the previous night. I promised, never to tell his secret. I was 19 then, and for the next two years, we had a similar arrangement. Every few weeks, he would come, drink himself silly, and sleep it off in my room. Eventually, it turned into more, and when I found I was pregnant with Louis, well, your father is nothing if not honorable. Imagine, to preserve my dignity, he made a simple barkeeper's daughter a queen."

Ferrand was shocked. He had never heard that story. He had spent so much time away from home during those years that he had no idea. He was having trouble believing it.

"That is why your father trusts me so much. He may not love me in the same way he loved your mother, but I have always been a good friend to him. He knows I will keep any secret he has. I do not pretend to know enough about politics or such matters to advise him, but he talks things over with me. And he always comes away with a solution of his own."

Ferrand had no idea his stepmother meant so much to his father. He was unsure of what to say.

"You know, Ferrand. The day you returned to the kingdom with Marya, I saw a light in your eyes, hers too. I thought to myself that you would have a long and happy marriage. The way she talked with your father over dinner. I knew she would be even better for you than I was for your father, because she was smart and understood politics. You could truly rely on her as an equal. Not to mention I could see that you are both extremely attracted to one another, and that never hurts."

Ferrand actually found himself blushing. His stepmother was describing everything he had ever hoped for in a wife, and what he knew to be true about his Marya.

"Thank you, Lila. You have given me a lot to think about. If you see Marya before I do, can you tell her that I would like to speak with her? Tell her I will find her this evening."

"Of course."

Ferrand wasn't sure what to make of his stepmother's words. He needed to think.

FERRAND STOOD AT THE window in one of the castle's lofty towers. He liked to go up there when he needed to think. Most people did not venture up there because it was a lot of steps to climb. Ferrand usually flew in the window.

He replayed his conversation with Lila in his mind. He had promised Marya to make her his equal, and she deserved it. How could he bear it if he lost her? And how could he risk leaving her and a potential child without him? One of them was bound to have their heart broken before the war was over. Was it worth it to let themselves have what time they could together in a true partnership?

Ferrand stared out the window. Geri was flying nearby. He watched her ducking and weaving in the sky, flying in pure joy. He had been so busy lately; he had been neglecting her, as well. Usually, they hunted together or flew together. Recently, they had barely seen each other.

Geri, he called.

Rand? she replied.

How are you?

Good

What should I do about everything, Ger? Should I go to war? he asked.

War is bad. Geri was amazingly intelligent for a bird, but she was still just a bird. He didn't know why he thought she would have answers for him.

I know war is bad, but it will come whether or not I fight. Should I help protect humans? He was not even sure why he was even asking. He knew he would protect them. But how could he protect the entire world, and his Marya at the same time? He could not deny he loved her, and he would not push her away again. It hadn't stopped him from falling for her in the first place, and it wouldn't protect them from war.

Like Marya, Geri interrupted his musings. Had she been reading his thoughts?

Yeah, I like her too. Ferrand replied.

Good mates. Have good babies.

Sure Geri, someday we will have good babies. He smirked, thinking to himself how much he would enjoy the process of creating them. He only wished they would not be bringing them into the turbulence of war. It did not seem fair to a child to do that. Yet, it was also imperative if he would guarantee their family line continue.

Babies soon, Geri replied. Ferrand's breathing stopped.

What do you mean, Babies soon? he asked.

Marya have babies soon.

How soon?

When they are ready.

Ferrand felt dizzy. He took several deep breaths.

Do you mean that Marya is- is- he had a hard time even thinking the word *pregnant?*

Yes.

How do you know? He asked.

Hear them. Like this. Like I hear you. Well not full thoughts. But murmers.

Marya was pregnant, and his familiar could hear the babies' thoughts? *Wait! Babies? As in more than one baby?*

Two babies.

Ferrand's head was spinning. They had only been together the one time. Of course, there was always a chance. But he hadn't expected—it's usually not that easy—or at least he thought.

Skies Above. He needed to talk to Marya. Did she know? She might not. It had only been about a month ago. When would she realize? Should he let her tell him when she did? Or should he tell her? This was not at all how things were supposed to happen. He would need to talk to his father and stepmother too. The wedding. Would it be soon enough that no one would suspect? Marya had been so worried about her reputation. He shouldn't have let her talk him into it that night.

Skies, they had already sent wedding invitations. They couldn't change them now. Would it be obvious at the wedding? Ferrand did not even know how long it took for a woman to carry a child. Damn it. This was a mess. Ferrand leaped out the tower window, summoning his wings as he dropped. He flew the rest of the way down to the ground and ran for the front door of the palace.

He should probably talk to Marya first, but he didn't know where she was, and he was not ready for that conversation, but he felt like he needed to speak to his father. His father was a lot of things, many of them not great. But he was also the most practical person Ferrand knew. He would advise him on the best way to handle the situation.

Skies, he had already been worried about her safety, but knowing she was carrying his child—no children—he suddenly felt overwhelmed with the need to hold and protect her. To stroke her hair and remind her how much he loved her. Had he ever even told her he loved her? Was this how his father had felt when his mother was carrying him, or with Lila and Louis? He had a hard time reconciling the flood of lovesick thoughts he was feeling with the image he had of his father.

Ferrand burst into his father's study without knocking. The king looked up at him from his desk, the look of annoyance on his face would have been comical if Ferrand had not been so desperate to talk to him.

"Father," he spoke. "I have something I need to discuss with you."

"I assumed as much. It is so desperate that you do not knock?"

"I am sorry, Father. My head is a bit of a mess."

"What has got my usually practical son in such an uproar?"

"Princess Marya."

"Not this still. Ferrand, your stepmother told me she talked to you."

"She did. But it's not—"

"Ferrand, I have not always been the kindest father, and I am sorry. But I love you, son. And I see the way you looked at Princess Marya. I have no regrets about my time with your mother."

"I know, that's what Lila told me. That's not—"

"It is better to hold on to love while you have it, even if it is fleeting as a dove."

Ferrand had never heard his father speak like that before. He remembered his father being happy with his mother, but he was never warm and fuzzy, even then.

"That's not what brought me here, though. Father. Princess Marya is—she is with child." He practically whispered the last word. It embarrassed him that he had allowed himself to get carried away, but after his conversation with his stepmother, he knew his father would understand.

"Well, that is a surprise. You've barely gone near the poor girl since you have arrived. When can you possibly have had time to? Well, no matter, it will certainly make it easier to ensure that you create an heir before you go off to command the navy."

His father's reaction was so calm. "That's part of the problem, father I can't leave her here alone, with a child. And once she knows about the war, she will want to help her kingdom."

"You do know that in the human kingdoms, having a child out of wedlock is a very big deal?"

"Yes, father. That's another part of the problem."

"As her legal guardian, her brother has every right to challenge you to a duel by the customs in the human kingdoms. Her family will be here in a week for the wedding."

"I know."

"Should I be worried?" his father asked.

"About Ivan? You have nothing to worry about from King Sova. I suspect his sisters have more balls between them than he has."

Ferrand heard a scuffling noise at the door. Skies above, if one of the servants had been in the hall and heard him talking—Marya had wanted so badly to preserve her reputation. Ferrand jumped up to see who it was. Maybe he could convince them to keep quiet.

When he opened the door, no one was there. He looked down the narrow hallway and caught a glimpse of a petite figure with long, brown hair, running at full speed, faster than any other human he knew. Skies, how much had she heard? She probably had not liked his insult toward her brother. He would have to go after her. The problem was, with her head start, and her Gift, he was not exactly sure he could catch up to her.

XXI

Marya

Marya had been looking everywhere for Ferrand. She had woken up from her nap and decided she needed to talk to him. Something was obviously going on with all the meetings he had been having with his father. He had promised she would be an equal in his life, and she would demand he fill her in on her what was going on.

She stalked to the palace and wandered around, looking for him. Finally, she ran into Queen Lila.

"Have you seen Ferrand?" she asked.

Queen Lila had the strangest smile on her face. "No, but he told me he wanted to talk to you, and he would find you this evening."

"I see. Well, if you see him before then. Tell him I also need to talk to him."

The queen's face broke out into an enormous grin. "Yes, of course. I will let him know."

Marya continued to search all the public places in the castle. She even braved knocking on his bedroom door. When she couldn't find him anywhere, she decided he must be holed up in yet another meeting with his father. She thought he had finished his meetings for the day when she saw him at the lake. If he was still with his father, she knew they wouldn't want to be interrupted, but she no longer cared. She would march in there and demand he tell her what was going on. She was tired of Ferrand and his father excluding her.

She paused outside the door to King Faucon's study, about to knock.

"Should I be worried?" She heard the king asking.

"Worried about Ivan?" Prince Ferrand asked. "You have nothing to worry about from King Sova. I think his sisters have more balls between them than he has."

Marya froze. They were discussing Ivan's ability—or lack thereof—in running his kingdom. Heat prickling behind her eyes, her heart sank. She knew Ferrand had known about Ivan's shortcomings, but she didn't think he would share that with his father. He knew how much she wanted to protect her kingdom. He had implied that his father was a wickedly selfish man who would take advantage of others' weaknesses. Was it all a lie, the things he had told her about helping her kingdom? Was this what all their meetings had been about? Tears threatened to fall from her eyes.

She should go in there and confront them both about their intentions towards her kingdom. Sniffing back her anger, she raised her hand to knock—and stopped herself.

She needed time to think. She wanted to be rational when she confronted them. If she went in their sniffling and bursting into tears, she would not look like the strong woman who could help her husband run his kingdom. She had maintained her composure thus far with Ferrand and his father. It wouldn't do to let that image crack.

Instead, Marya did what she always did when she was not ready to face something. She ran.

Marya took off down the hall and out the front door as fast as her legs could take her. She did not pause when she hit the outdoors; she just ran. Faster and faster. She wished she could run all the way home to Selmy Island. She would make Ivan listen to her. Make the councilors let her help. Warn them that her father-in-law was a selfish bastard that would take advantage of them.

It was foolish to pretend she could run to Selmy Island, but she would just keep running until she couldn't run anymore. She barely looked where she was going. She hadn't realized it, but during the time she had been in Southshore, her legs had memorized the palace grounds. She passed the furthest outbuildings and the stables, bursting through the meadow that led towards the lake where she had watched Ferrand swim. She ran until she had gone further and faster than she ever had before.

Marya laughed at the thought that she truly was running away from one of her suitors. She had laughed at the thought forever ago. The day of her parents' death when Ivan had first insisted she would be getting married. Had it only been two months ago? She barely remembered that day. She still had not stopped to process it.

If her father was still alive, they wouldn't be in this mess. She would be by his side, helping as she always had.

She felt the first tear trickle down her cheek at the thought of her father.

If her father was still here, she reminded herself, she might not have made a marriage alliance with Southshore. She would not have known what it was to be treated as an equal—even if it had all been a sham. She would still be following her father around like a puppy, and nothing would be any different. Her father couldn't live forever, and no one would let her do anything useful anyway.

How had her mother been able to stand sitting on the sidelines and letting her father do everything? Her mother was just as smart as Marya was and just as passionate. Marya wished she could be with her right then. While she had never been as close to her mother as her father, she would have given anything to feel her mother's arms wrapped around her, giving her advice and telling her it would all be ok.

Maybe her mother could explain why Ferrand was amazing one minute but distant and cold the next. The tears were flowing faster now. She could hardly see where she was going. Could hardly think. Could hardly breathe.

When the soft grass gave way to harder stone, she didn't even notice. Her grief had her too wrapped up to care.

And then she was screaming. She shrieked as the ground fell away from her. She had run too far. Marya tumbled end over end down a steeply sloping stone precipice. She landed with a loud crack, and her screaming stopped as the wind was knocked completely out of her. Marya lay half on her back, half on her side, gulping for air. She was so stunned she did not move.

Marya stared at the clear blue sky. The ledge that marked the edge of the palace plateau was far above. Marya willed her lungs to work properly, and eventually, she sucked in a large gulp of air. Marya took several deep, steadying breaths before even trying to move. When she tried to push herself up to sitting, pain lanced through her right arm. It would not support any weight, and she realized her wrist was bent at an unnatural angle.

Marya took several deep breaths. She needed to roll to her other side, but she didn't know how much space surrounded her on the ledge. She knew she had not fallen far from the top of the plateau, and she had no idea how steep the cliff was the rest of the way down. Warily, she reached behind her back with her uninjured arm, feeling for the edge of the ledge. When her fingers met with only stone, she inched backward. Alternating between reaching with her hand, and scootching her body back, Marya wormed her way across the flat stone until she felt air with her outstretched arm.

She breathed a sigh of relief. The stone shelf was wide enough that she should be able to roll over. Her arm was throbbing with all the crawling she had done. She decided it would be safer to roll back the way she'd come, towards the plateau. It would force her over the injured arm, but it still seemed safer than wriggling her way across the ledge and then rolling towards the cliff edge, hoping she had left enough space that she wouldn't roll off.

Marya gritted her teeth against the onslaught of pain she knew was about to feel. Using her good arm for leverage, she pushed off the stone behind her, flipping onto her front. She groaned as pain shot through her right shoulder. Her entire arm went numb, and her vision blacked out.

WHEN MARYA OPENED HER eyes again, she was unsure how long she had been unconscious, but the sun was significantly lower in the sky. Lying face down on the stone rock, she cried. What could she possibly do about her situation? She hated being helpless. She had fought her entire life to prove she was as capable as Ivan. Harsh sobs wracked her body, sending twinges of pain through her injured arm.

Ever since Prince Ferrand came into her life, she had been making a fool out of herself. She had sworn to stay and assist Ivan with the kingdom, but it really had not taken much effort from Prince Ferrand to agree to marry him. On the ship, she had let him turn her into one of those simpering girls, jumping into his bed and batting her lashes at him like a proper idiot. Not that he hadn't given her plenty of opportunities to stop, making her reassure him at every step she was certain it was what she wanted.

Then he had promised her to be an equal in his kingdom, and she had not fought him to include her in whatever it was that was going on. Why had she been so stupid?

Because she loved him. She knew it was true. She had trusted him. He had taken care of her and shown her he cared about her. And her kingdom. She thought he would protect her and her people, and it had felt so nice to let go of her worries for even just a brief time. To let someone else worry about her. To think that she did not have to do it all on her own. Everyone needed help from time to time. If anyone would be that person for her, she had thought it might be Ferrand.

Then he betrayed her. Marya clenched her uninjured hand into a fist. Heat coursed through her veins in a way she had never experienced before. Ferrand had sold her out to his father, whom she had thought he hated.

And as usual, when it came down to it, she was a coward. She hadn't stood up for herself. Instead, she had run. The tears were flowing harder now. She could not run this time. There was nowhere to run. She had to figure out a way to solve the problem.

Marya pushed herself up with her good arm. She reached up the side of the cliff. There was no way she could reach the top. She dug her fingers into the dirt. Her wrist screamed in protest. How was she going to climb a sheer cliff face with only one arm? It was hopeless.

She screamed as loud as she could in pure frustration.

And her scream came echoing back. Only it wasn't her scream. It was different. It was—

Marya sobbed in relief when she saw the enormous falcon sore over her head.

Geri circled down to where she stood and nudged her with her head. Marya hugged the falcon tight to her chest and cried into her feathers.

XXII

Ferrand

Ferrand felt a weight in his chest lift at the sound of Geri's shrill cry.

Marya? He thought at her.

Marya here, Geri replied.

Ferrand followed the sound of Geri's cry. He had been searching on foot so he wouldn't miss her, but now that he knew where to head, he summoned his wings to get there as quickly as possible.

His heart squeezed in his chest as he came closer to the edge of the plateau, realizing where she must be.

He couldn't look. *Is she all right?* He asked Geri.

Yes. She replied.

Ferrand flew out over the precipice, spotting Marya and Geri on a small ledge about a third of the way down the side of the rock face. How had she wound up there? It was a wonder she was not severely hurt. He let out a sigh of relief that she seemed relatively unharmed—until he remembered that she was carrying his children. Panic struck him like a blow to the gut, and he swooped down to the ledge at top speed. Marya had her arms wrapped around Geri's neck, and she was sobbing.

"What in the name of the Winds were you thinking?" He shouted. "We have been searching for you all evening. Even Geri did not see which way you went. How could you be so foolish to run out here without thinking where you were?"

Marya didn't even look at him. Just continued crying into Geri's feathers.

Be nice, Rand. Geri admonished him.

She was right. He should not be shouting at her. He should hold her close and never let go. She looked like she didn't want anything to do with him. She refused to look at him, clinging to his bird.

"I want to return to Selmy," she whispered.

Ferrand's heart shattered. Had he ruined things so badly then? He needed to fix it. He did not know how.

"Please do not go," he begged. His voice cracked with pain at the thought of losing her, especially now with the babies. The babies!

Geri, can you tell if the babies are all right?

Still hear babies. Thank the Skies! Of course, Geri was no doctor. But if she could still hear them, that had to be a good sign. He would have to tell Marya about the babies. But he hated to use it to force her to stay with him. He wouldn't do that to her. He needed to convince her she wanted to stay—with him.

"I have to go. I cannot stay here with you, knowing you are only after my kingdom—and not me." She whispered the last part, and Ferrand heard the hurt in her voice. Did she really believe that?

"Marya, look at me," he begged. She did not budge. "Please look at me." Begrudgingly, she let go of his bird. The slow speed at which she turned towards him felt like an eternity. When she, at last, looked at him, he continued. "Why would you think I am only interested in your kingdom? I don't even want to rule my kingdom. What would I do with yours?"

"Do not lie to me, Ferrand!" She spat. "I heard you and your father, in his study, discussing my brother's inability to rule."

"What are you talking about?" He honestly did not understand what she meant. "We weren't discussing that at all. We were discussing the arrival of your family next week for the wedding."

"But your father asked if you expected trouble, and you said Ivan had no balls."

Ferrand dropped his head in his hands. He stifled a laugh. Had that really been what had sent her running. He had figured she was mad at the insult, but then he thought when she disappeared, it must have been something worse. He never thought he had caused her to worry. He would betray her kingdom!

"Is that all you heard of our conversation?" he asked, a hint of humor in his voice.

"Isn't it enough?" she asked. "And why do you seem about to laugh?"

"Marya, sit down. Let's talk. You misunderstood completely. Though without the context, I can understand. I was not discussing—Oh, how do I tell you this?" Marya sat, her expression evidence that she was skeptical of what he would say. How would he tell her? Men were not supposed to be the ones to break this news.

Marya stared at him, waiting for an explanation. Ferrand reached over and took her hand in his. She looked about to pull it back, but she stopped herself. "You are... we are... I mean..." he trailed off. Ferrand cleared this throat and tried again. "Marya, you are with child. My child. Children, actually."

"What?" Marya asked, a look of disbelief coming over her face. "What are you talking about? How?"

"Marya, please tell me you knew enough to know that it was possible when—" Ferrand stopped, noticing the blush that crept over her.

"Yes, of course, I understand how that all works. I told you as much that night in the cave." she snapped at him. That was right. She had said something about an aunt. "But how do you know that? And what has that to do with Ivan?"

"Geri told me. Apparently, she could sense their thoughts, the same way she senses mine."

"I'm—I'm really going to have a baby. Did you say babies?" she asked.

"Yes. Twins Marya! We are going to have twins." He suddenly felt giddy at the thought. But worry returned as Marya kept staring at him incredulously. She did not speak.

"Marya. Please say something," He whispered.

"I am not even sure I know where to begin. I mean, I knew it could—but it was only once. Skies, Ferrand. I'm barely old enough to be a mother."

"You are the same age my mother was when I was born," Ferrand commented. "Oh, please tell me you are at least somewhat happy. I felt a shock at first when Geri told me. But I find now, more than anything, I am excited."

"You still have not answered my other question. What does this any of it have to do with Ivan?"

"My father thought your brother might challenge me to a duel over your honor," Ferrand replied.

"I suppose he could." And then she let out a small chuckle. "No, you are completely right. He might feel he ought to, but Ivan would never have the balls to do it. As long as he knows I'm happy, he will be fine."

"*Are* you happy?" Ferrand asked.

"I honestly don't know how I feel. It's like I want to be happy. I wasn't exactly ready for this, but I knew it would come someday. But I am still furious with you."

"Furious with me?" he asked. He knew things had been distant between them, but what could he have done to make her furious? Now that she knew he wasn't plotting to take over her kingdom.

"You promised me. You told me I would be your partner, your equal. Ever since we arrived in Southshore, your father—whom I thought you hated, by the way—has kept you tied up in meetings all day. You haven't given one bit of input in anything to do with the wedding, leaving me alone with your stepmother for hours on end. You're keeping something from me. Every time I ask about your meetings, you change the subject."

Relief flooded him. This was something he could fix. His stepmother had been right. He could trust Marya completely.

"Marya," he spoke. "I am so sorry. I have been terrible to you. I know that I cannot go back and undo what was done, but please let me explain where I was coming from."

Marya glared at him.

"That night we shared on the ship. I told you about why I was afraid to get close to you. Once I let myself, however. When I realized I was falling in love with you—"

"You're what?" she interrupted him.

"I am in love with you, Marya, and it terrifies me. Now that I have accepted that I love you, I cannot help but desire to protect you. I do not want to lose you. Marya, I promise I will tell you everything that is going on—after we get you back to the palace and have a doctor check you over."

"I am fine," she replied.

"I am so relieved you are fine. But I will never stop worrying about you now that I've come to love you."

"Oh, Ferrand. I don't know what to say."

"Say you love me, too. Or at least that you think you can grow to," he begged.

"Ferrand, I love you, too. I think I loved you from the moment you held me in your arms, comforting me from a nightmare. I had never let anyone care for me that way, and you made me feel safe in a way I had never felt before."

"I am so sorry, my love. I have been an idiot."

"Promise me. Please include me in whatever affairs you are involved in. I want to help. I want to be involved. I want to be your partner in all aspects of your life."

"Only if you promise me, you will not try to do everything all by yourself. And you will not senselessly put yourself into danger?"

Marya nodded. "I never learned to ask for help. Well, I will start by asking for your help right now. Ferrand, can you please get me off this ledge?"

Ferrand pulled her towards him and kissed her on the nose. Marya winced at his hand on her shoulder.

"You're hurt? You said you were fine. Geri said you were fine." Panic gripped Ferrand again, cold running through his veins.

"*I am fine*. I think I might have dislocated my shoulder and maybe broke my wrist. Really considering my fall. It's nothing." Then it was Marya's turn for fear to flood her face. "The babies?" she asked as if it had just dawned on her.

"Geri can still hear them. We will call a doctor as soon as we get back to the palace. I am going to pick you up now. I will try not to move your arm too much."

Ferrand scooped her into his arm, cradling her close to him. He never wanted to let go.

"Are you all right?" he asked.

"No," she replied.

"What is it?" he asked.

"This is the first time you have held me in weeks, and I missed hav—"

Ferrand leaned down and kissed her soundly on the lips. Electricity stirred in his veins, but this kiss was different than the others they had shared. He poured all the love he felt for her into the kiss, and she gobbled it up, returning it with her own. When they broke apart, he felt that he was the luckiest man alive.

XXIII

Marya

Everything was a blur after Ferrand flew her back to the palace. Marya vaguely remembered being hungry, and someone brought her something to eat. She remembered everyone in the palace fussing over her. Even the King came to make sure she was all right. Possibly he was still worried about Ivan's reaction to everything she had been through.

Someone called a doctor. She was right that she broke her wrist and dislocated her shoulder in the fall. She had a vague memory of the blinding pain when the doctor set her wrist. She may have even passed out again. The doctor wrapped her wrist with a splint so it would heal properly and put her arm in a sling. Everyone kept telling her how lucky she was that it wasn't worse. She couldn't relax, however, until she knew that her babies were all right.

At first, it had stunned her when Ferrand told her she was pregnant. However, the longer she thought about the two life forms growing inside of her, she was becoming accustomed to the idea. It was amazing to think she and Ferrand had created new life together. She loved her babies already.

"Marya," Ferrand called into her room. "Are you awake?"

That was another thing. The pain tonic she had been drinking left her drowsy. She had been in and out of sleep. She did not even know what day it was. "Yes. I am awake," she called.

"The midwife is here."

Ferrand entered the room with a middle-aged woman with a severe black bun and wrinkles around her eyes.

"My dear," the older woman greeted her as she entered. "I have no magic to assess your situation fully. The prince's pet is probably better equipped to tell you at this point how your babies are doing."

Marya nodded. "She can hear them."

"How far along do you think you are, dear?"

Marya felt her face heat.

"Oh, come child. I have been delivering babies for many years and have three children of my own. Let's not be coy here. I know how you came to be in this situation, and I make no judgment. I just need to know approximately what point in the pregnancy you are at."

"Around a month," Ferrand supplied when she failed to answer again. Marya smiled at him gratefully. She noticed he was wringing his hands together and looked about ready to jump out of his skin. Marya smiled at him, hoping to be reassuring, but her insides felt like they were twisting in knots.

"You are sure?" the midwife asked.

Marya nodded her head.

"It is too soon for me to know much. I would not have even known you were with child until you realized it yourself. Soon, you will most likely get frequently sick to your stomach. It shouldn't last more than a few months before you feel well again."

Marya and Ferrand listened intently to the midwife's instructions, promising to call her right away if Marya experienced any of the worrying signs she talked about. It relieved Marya to know she could continue to run for a while yet, as long as she was careful and did not go near any more cliffs.

When the midwife had gone, Ferrand climbed up on the bed next to her.

"What are you doing?" she asked. "You should not even be in here without a chaperon."

"I think we are past the point of pretending that I have not despoiled you."

Marya felt herself blushing.

"I cannot wait until your arm heals?"

"Why is that?" Marya asked.

"Because I would like to despoil you again. And again. At this point, I've already ruined your reputation. So, I do not see why we have to wait anymore."

Marya felt a jolt of heat prickle inside her. She gazed up at Ferrand. It had been so long since they had been together—almost a month.

Ferrand's eyes had darkened to the color of the sea again as he looked down at her. Marya's heart was racing, but she couldn't forget that he was still keeping things from her. If they were going to make things work between them, they needed to be honest with each other.

"You know," she purred, "I think we could find a way to make that work, without hurting my arm further—"

Ferrand's breath was coming faster against her cheek.

"—But first, I need you to tell me what in the name of the Gods is going on that you've been hiding from me? You promised me I could be your partner in everything. Was that just some promise to get convince me to agree to this marriage or to get me into your bed?"

"Of course not!" he replied.

"Then tell me!"

"Fine. You're right. I'm sorry. You should know this. It's selfish of me to keep it from you," he said.

Marya raised an eyebrow, waiting for him to continue.

"There will be a war. I don't know when. But King Nasir had inside information from a fae connection of his in Azria. There are many Dark Fae who are plotting to release a Dark Fae monstrosity that has been bound since the first war. Somehow the plot begins with the Azrian Kingdom invading surrounding kingdoms. He does not yet know how they plan to release Deathless, as he is sometimes called, but he is certain it will happen."

"But what does that have to do with invading other kingdoms?" she asked, her heart clenched, thinking of how close Selmy Island was to Azria.

"King Nasir believes that the Azrian king is in alliance with the Dark Fae who wish to free this Deathless. They are looking for something. Nazir knows not what, but that they cannot find it within Azria."

Her horror must have been evident on her face because Ferrand was pulling her close and murmuring into her hair, "We will find a way to protect Selmy."

"We? As in you and me? You promise you will let me be involved this time."

Ferrand did not answer her, stroking her hair and holding her against his warm frame. She was relieved he had climbed into the bed on her uninjured side. Leaning into his warm embrace gave her the feeling that everything would be alright somehow. He was her partner, and whatever happened next, it was not on her shoulders alone as she had always imagined.

"My father thinks that I should head to Selmy and offer my services to your brother," he finally spoke. "I could bring my ship and others from my kingdom to bolster his navy."

That had been one of her uncle's biggest concerns, their navy falling apart without her father's leadership. "Yes, that makes sense. We have a sizable armada, but Ivan knows nothing about commanding a naval fleet."

"Do you suppose he will accept my help?" Ferrand asked.

"I will make him." Other than her wish to remain unmarried, Ivan had never questioned her before. "Though, I think he knows he needs all the help he can get. Last I saw him, he was practically begging the council to take the pressure off of him."

"Good," Ferrand replied.

His hand stilled in her hair, and his body slumped against hers. Marya looked up into his face. He was frowning. Apart from their emotional talk, that night on the ship, she had never seen him wear such an expression.

"What's wrong?" she asked.

"I don't wish to leave you. The thought of leaving you alone and possibly missing the birth of the babies—no. I want to be there for that."

"My family will be here for the wedding soon enough. You can make plans with Ivan then. And when the time comes to go to Selmy, take me with you." she said.

"Take you with me? Into a war? With infants?"

"No. Not into the war. But take me to Selmy. You promised to involve me. If you bring me into war council meetings as your equal, Ivan's stuffy old council cannot keep me out. I would love to see old Digby's face when you defer to me for ideas." She laughed.

"But, I will still have to leave you eventually. If there is actual warfare at sea, I will have to go out into it."

"A least I will be with my sisters. I will not be alone. And they can help me with the babies." She found herself grinning at the idea of being with her family and still being close to Ferrand.

"Do you promise you will keep yourself and the little ones out of danger? You will not go marching into battle with a baby at the breast."

"I promise. But can you imagine if I marched into a council meeting with one? Those stuffy old men might die of heart failure on the spot."

Ferrand chuckled, cradling Marya's head to his chest. "All right," he said. "You can come with me. We will figure this out—together." He kissed her on the top of the head, and she nuzzled into him. Considering she had just learned of a coming war, it surprised her how light her heart felt.

"I love you," Marya said into his chest.

Ferrand squeezed her. She could tell he was being careful not to jostle her arm. Snaking her hand up to curve around his neck, she lifted her face to him for a kiss. Her prince obliged, pressing his soft, warm mouth against her own.

Marya sighed into the kiss, which Ferrand deepened. The kiss was different from their previous kisses—softer, sweeter, yet no less passionate. Tongues tangled together in long, languid strokes, and jolts of electricity ran down Marya's spine.

His soft silky hair tangled in her fingers, she pressed herself against him.

Ferrand pulled his lips away from hers. The sudden coldness where his mouth had been caused her to shiver.

"Why did you stop?" she asked, her voice coming out breathy and high.

"If you keep kissing me like that, I will not be able to hold back from loving you fully."

"And why should you hold back?" she asked, arching her back towards him.

"I don't want to hurt you," he replied.

"So be gentle. My arm is injured, not my entire body. Please, Ferrand, I have missed your touch this past month. I cannot wait another month until the wedding," she begged.

"You would like that, would you?" he asked in a low, raspy voice.

Marya bit her lip and nodded her head.

"Lay down, flat on your back," he growled the command.

Obliging, Marya rolled out of his embrace until she lay flat on her back. She did not feel so attractive with her arm bandaged and held in a sling.

Ferrand did not seem to mind. She could see the lust in his eyes as he propped himself up on one arm next to her. "Where should I touch you first?" he murmured, his voice a silken caress, sending shivers down her body.

How was she supposed to respond?

"Should I touch you here?" his voice was barely a whisper as he settled his warm, callused hand on her hip. She was wearing only a thin cotton nightdress, and she felt tingly at his touch.

Marya nodded again.

"Or I could touch you here." Ferrand slid his hand slowly down the side of her thigh and started bunching her nightdress up until the soft fabric was only covering half of her leg. Marya's breath hitched in her throat as Ferrand pulled the fabric up higher and higher, baring almost her entire leg and settling his hand just above her knee.

Marya waited, but Ferrand did not move his hand. What was he doing now? Ferrand was staring at her expectantly, but he did not move. Marya squirmed under his gaze.

"All right," she finally pleaded. "Keep touching me, please."

"Where?" he whispered.

"I don't know."

"You know what you want, Marya. Tell me where to touch you."

Marya took a deep breath and closed her eyes. "You could—you could move your hand a bit higher," she breathed out in a rush. She knew her cheeks were flaming.

Ferrand inched his hand up her leg, rough calluses tickling her skin. An aching desire stirred in her belly and spread between her legs. She wanted him to touch her there, but she wasn't sure if she could get the words out.

"Higher," her voice came out in a barely audible whisper. "Please."

Ferrand obeyed, his hand gliding up to the top of her thigh, his fingertips just barely grazing across her most sensitive parts. Once, twice, and then his hand skirted away to rest on her hip, under her nightdress, leaving her wanting more.

"Please, Ferrand," she begged.

"Please what?" he asked in a low rumble.

She opened her eyes and looked at him. His face was a mask of complete control. How was he able to keep so calm when she felt like she was on fire?

"You know what I want," she squeaked out.

"I want you to say it."

"Please touch me—between my legs."

Ferrand moved his hand so slowly across her abdomen she thought she would scream. Then just as slowly he slid it down, down, down, and when he finally touched her where she wanted him to, Marya nearly cried out in relief.

"Is this what you wanted?" he growled, bringing his lips right next to her ear.

"Yes," she breathed. Ferrand continued to pleasure her with his skilled fingers. Marya writhed beneath him. Her entire body was on fire.

"You are the most amazing woman I have ever met," Ferrand said. His hot breath tickled her ear, and she arched into him.

The angle was awkward, but Marya reached for his trousers. Ferrand swatted her hand away.

"There will be time for that when you are healed. I plan to make love to you as often as you will let me for the next hundred years, maybe more."

Marya looked up at him, her mouth open, and an eyebrow raised. Humans did not live for hundreds of years. What was he talking about? Her confusion must have been apparent in her face, because he replied, "I forgot to tell you. If we win this war, I get to take you to the fae realm, where we can be life-bonded in a way that will match our lifespans so we may live out our lives together into old age.

What? Marya tried to process what he was saying, but he had dipped his fingers inside her, and her thoughts muddled together. Marya's heart rate and breathing increased. She gasped and moaned as he alternated between plunging and stroking until at last, her body went first taut, then shattered into a million pieces as her climax broke over her.

When her body had calmed down, and her breathing slowed, she opened her eyes to find Ferrand gazing down at her with a look of wonderment on his face.

"I will never tire of seeing you come undone like that," he said. "I love you, Marya. I cannot wait to make you my wife and to spend the rest of my life with you."

That jogged her memory. "Did you say that in the fae realm, I will be able to be with you into your old age?"

Ferrand nodded his head. He had tears in his eyes, and his smile stretched across his entire face. It had thrilled her to spend forty or fifty more years with him, but one hundred seemed too good to be true.

Ferrand leaned down and kissed her on the forehead. "I love you, Marya. Get some rest. Lila will have a fit if you must wear that sling to the wedding ceremony.

Marya chuckled. "I love you, too," she replied, sensing that her answering smile was as wide as his. She wanted him to stay with her, but she could feel the sleepiness of the pain medicine taking hold.

Epilogue

Olga

"Marya!" Anna squealed, "You look beautiful!"

Olga had to agree. Her older sister was practically glowing as her maid, Ellie, was stuffing her into her wedding gown—a gorgeous pale green dress, fitted through the beaded bodice and flaring out into a wide bell with a train. It was hard to imagine that practical, independent Marya, was not only getting married, but she was happy about it. When Marya had left Selmy Island with Prince Ferrand, she had been furious at their brother and their uncle for insisting she marry. Olga felt herself smiling at her sister's happiness.

Anna was hugging their sister, and Olga could see Marya wince slightly at their baby sister's rough embrace. Olga still couldn't believe the story Marya had told them about how she had come to be injured. Thank the Winged Ones that it hadn't been worse.

"Hold on," Ellie instructed, pointing towards the bed with a scowl. "You are not fitting into your gown."

Olga had to stifle a chuckle at the maid's disapproving glare at her mistress. Marya grunted and gripped her bedpost while Ellie tugged harder on the laces of Marya's corset. "Please, Ellie," she gasped out. "You're going to make me sick."

"Ack. Everything makes you sick." Ellie replied.

Olga watched the interaction between her sister and the maid. Why was Ellie so annoyed? And why was Marya always sick? Marya couldn't be—No, not her practical sister.

When Marya was at last laced into her dress, Ellie sat her on the stool in front of her dressing table. Marya appeared to be having difficulty breathing in the tight gown, but she gritted her teeth and smiled at her sisters in the mirror.

"I still cannot believe Ivan didn't come," Marya complained. It had been quite the commotion when the ship from Selmy arrived with only the two princesses and some courtiers aboard. The queen had arranged everything so that Ivan and Olga would be paired together for the ceremony and dinner, and Anna would be paired with Prince Ferrand's younger brother, Louis.

"Ivan didn't come because he is an idiot," Anna piped up, from where she had made herself comfortable on Marya's bed.

"Anna," Olga scolded. Though she tended to agree with her sister's sentiment, they had agreed they wouldn't tell Marya how bad it had gotten with Ivan. Marya had always felt responsible for running the kingdom, and they had decided not to worry her now that she was about to be married.

"Oh, Ivan is Ivan," Olga responded. "He still has his nose in a book most of the time, but I think he is settling into his role a bit more." It wasn't an outward lie, he was settling in, but only because Uncle Tavar was essentially doing his job for him.

"I still wish he had come. The King is anxious to speak with him."

"Well, I suppose we will have to bring a message back to him," Olga replied.

"Oh, let's not talk about all that. This is your wedding day," Anna cut in. "We want to hear about you. You've barely told us anything. How do you like your new kingdom? Tell us about your prince."

"Well, you know. I didn't want to leave Selmy at all, but the more I got to know Ferrand-" she trailed off, a pretty blush staining her cheeks. Olga had never thought to see the day sensible, independent Marya would be blushing over a man.

"You look so happy!" Anna squealed. "Oh, he seems just dreamy. What's he really like? Have you kissed him?"

Marya's blush deepened.

"You have kissed him!" Anna cried.

The way Marya averted her gaze, Olga was starting to wonder if she'd done more than kiss him. The reproving frown on Ellie's face as she twisted and yanked at Marya's hair only served to convince her further that Marya and her prince had not kept their relationship innocent. Marya! Marya, who was always thinking ahead and planning. She was the responsible one.

"Actually," Marya said, "It's probably good Ivan didn't come. I have to tell you something, and he would not be happy."

"What?" Anna asked excitedly.

"Promise not to tell Ivan?"

"Yes, of course," Olga replied.

"I am with child," Marya practically whispered.

"You're going to have a baby?" Anna squealed.

"Ow!" Marya shouted at Ellie, who was tugging her hair harder.

"Two, actually. I am having twins."

Olga was in shock. How had her pragmatic older sister gotten into that situation outside of marriage? She supposed, even Marya was allowed to be impulsive sometimes. She mentally did the math. It had only been two months since Marya left home. How could she possibly know already she was having twins?

She was about to ask just that when Marya continued, "Prince Ferrand's Falcon is a fae creature. They can communicate telepathically."

Well, that was new and interesting. "Like Anna?" Olga asked.

"It's different. It's a connection between the two of them. A bond. It's apparently common for fae and demi-fae to have a bond like that with an animal. They call them familiars. Anyway, it's a bit different because they can have actual conversations. And Geri, that's the falcon, can hear the babies the same way she can hear Ferrand."

"But what in the world would babies be thinking of?" Olga asked.

"She says it's not coherent thoughts like you or I would have, more just a dull murmuring sound that comes and goes from time to time."

"I wonder if I could hear it if I tried," Anna said.

"Why, I don't know! There isn't anyone here with a Gift like that, so I hadn't thought of that."

"Can I try?" Anna asked, hopping off the bed and rushing to her sister.

"I don't see why not."

Olga watched as Anna closed her eyes, placing a hand on Marya's belly. She didn't need to touch the person whose thoughts she was sensing, but she had told them once that it helped. Anna didn't use her Gift often because it often left her feeling sick to her stomach when she used it.

"I definitely hear something," she said, excitedly jumping up from Marya's side. "It is, it's almost like someone mumbling under their breath, and no words can be understood. Oh, Marya, I wish we could stay until the babies are born. I want to see them."

"That's what we needed to talk to Ivan about. Ferrand and I are planning to come to Selmy after the babies are born. Oh. Ivan should be here. I will have to fill you two in, and you will have to tell him."

"Tell him what?" Olga asked.

Marya filled them in on what she had learned about a war brewing between different factions of fae that were still living among humans on the western continent of Dudaimash. Olga hadn't realized there were so many more fae in the human realm there. She hadn't known any of the Dark Fae had remained in their realm after the last great Fae war. The world had been ripped apart by the calamity, and Olga shuddered at the thought that it could happen again. If the Dark Fae returned to power, and if the Gates to the fae realm could be re-opened, what would that mean for the humans?

Olga and Anna promised to talk to Ivan, just as Queen Lila entered the room.

"You girls look lovely," she exclaimed.

"Thank you," they chorused.

"Olga, I have arranged for King Nasir to escort you down the aisle and sit with you as a dinner partner. It will balance out our numbers."

Olga nodded to the queen, trying not to groan. She had heard terrible things about the warrior king from Wendyl. Thank the Winged, it would only be one dinner and entering the ceremony together.

"All right, come along girls. It's time," Queen Lila chirped.

The ceremony was to be held by the lake on the palace grounds.

When they reached the entryway of the palace, two men were waiting for them. Well, one man and one boy. Louis Faucon was a younger version of Ferrand and their father. He watched them as they entered the room. Olga assumed the other man who stood studying a painting on the wall must be King Nasir.

Louis blushed as he offered his arm to Anna. Too bad he wasn't a few years older. Anna was envious of Marya's handsome fairy prince. She and Louis could be cute together if he was a bit older. No matter. Beautiful, sweet, charming Anna would have her pick of any husband when the time came. Olga made her way to King Nasir's side and cleared her throat.

He turned to face her, and Olga's world dropped out from under her feet. This man—was he considered a man if he was one hundred percent fae?—was the most breathtakingly handsome being she had ever encountered. Her heart hammering in her chest, she tried to speak but could only manage to stare at him. His short golden locks were wavy and messy in a casual way that did not strike her as kingly. She trailed her eyes down his face, noting the sharp points of his ears and the sharp chiseled jawline. Gods, he was perfection. And Olga felt her face heating.

With a lack of any expression—except perhaps boredom—he proffered his arm to her with a slight nod of his head. Her heart leaped when she placed her hand on his muscled forearm.

As they made their way out to the lake, Anna chatted amicably with Louis, and the queen continued to talk to Marya about the dinner arrangements and the ball that was to follow. King Nasir said nothing. He looked straight ahead with the same uninterested look on his insanely handsome face. Walking in silence, she found herself wondering what types of things might bring a smile to his full sensual lips. Gods! What was happening to her? Thank the Winged, they were almost at the lake.

Olga pasted a pleasant smile on her face as they walked past the crowds of people who had turned up to see the wedding. The Faucons were loved by their people, and it seemed the entire kingdom had wanted to see their beloved prince marry the beautiful foreign princess. Olga's skin prickled with the attention focused on her and King Nasir. Of course, everyone would be looking at the gorgeous fae king. She tried to shrink into his shadow. It was a relief when they reached the end of the aisle, and they split apart to their places.

Anna and Louis were drawing just as much attention as they finished their descent down the aisle. Anna was smiling prettily at all the guests, waving and batting her lashes. Olga rolled her eyes. The young prince, on the other hand, kept stealing furtive glances at Anna and blushing, until they parted ways. Anna stood next to Olga, and Louis made his way, to stand between Ferrand and Nasir.

Then Marya stepped into view. Olga had never seen her sister so happy. She would have believed she had become one of the Fae the way she glowed. An enormous smile lit up her face. Olga sneaked a glance at Prince Ferrand. His answering smile was just as effervescent. Olga thanked the Gods that her sister had found such happiness. The only sour note to it all was knowing that in just a few days, she and Anna would be returning to Selmy without her and that it would be up to them to help Ivan navigate what was to come. She would not think about that during the wedding though. She would concentrate all her love and energy on her sister and how happy she was.

The Story Continues with Olga in Eagle's Embrace

PERFECT FOR FANS OF Bridgerton and Sarah J Maas alike, the Princesses of Selmy Island series features all your favorite historical romance tropes in a vivid fantasy setting on the brink of a fae war.

Each book contains a standalone romance that can technically be read separately, but they are better read in order to follow the full story of the fae war.

A Human Princess with a Wish to Remain Invisible

Princess Olga Sova spent most of her life as the invisible sister, which suited her just fine. Unfortunately, her older brother, Ivan, is mucking up the kingdom now that he is king, and her older sister has gone off to marry her true love. With the balance of their family thrown off, Olga needs to help her Ivan find his place as king. She thinks the best way to do this is to find him a queen. Unfortunately, when she puts the idea in his head to throw a ball to find a suitable bride, he gets it in his own head that it would be the perfect setting to find her a husband. She always knew she would marry for politics, but with her two left feet, a ball is the last place she will catch a husband.

A Fae King Separated from His Beloved Homeland

The novelty of ruling a human kingdom has worn off for King Nasir after more than a century. All he wants now is to return to the fae realm where he belongs. For the first time since the Gates were sealed, leaving him trapped in the human realm, it is looking like this is a real possibility. The only problem is, to make it happen, he needs to play nice with the humans so they can win the coming war. He even agrees to attend a human ball and convince a princess to marry one of his men.

At the Sova's royal ball, Olga and Nasir find themselves caught in a compromising position. Now King Nasir must marry Princess Olga or her brother will pull his support from the war efforts. And to make matters worse, his chief advisor thinks a human queen in his kingdom will also win his support with his own people.

Will they be able to set aside their difference to make a union work for the good of both of their kingdoms?

Eagle's Embrace is available in paperback, on Kindle, and Kindle Unlimited.

TO RECEIVE EXCLUSIVE content, including short stories, deleted scenes, and access a steamy, fake-dating, Rapunzel retelling, *Belleflower*, sign up for my newsletter at http://mandirichards.com/subscribe

If you liked this book, or even if you did not, please considering leaving a review for Falcon's Kiss on Amazon and anywhere else you review books. Independent authors rely on our readers' reviews to help our book get visibility among the thousands upon thousands of books on Amazon.

And if you can't get enough of me, consider following me on social media. You can find me on facebook Instagram and tiktok @mandi.richards.writes. I share snippets, behind the scenes stuff, and lots of silliness.

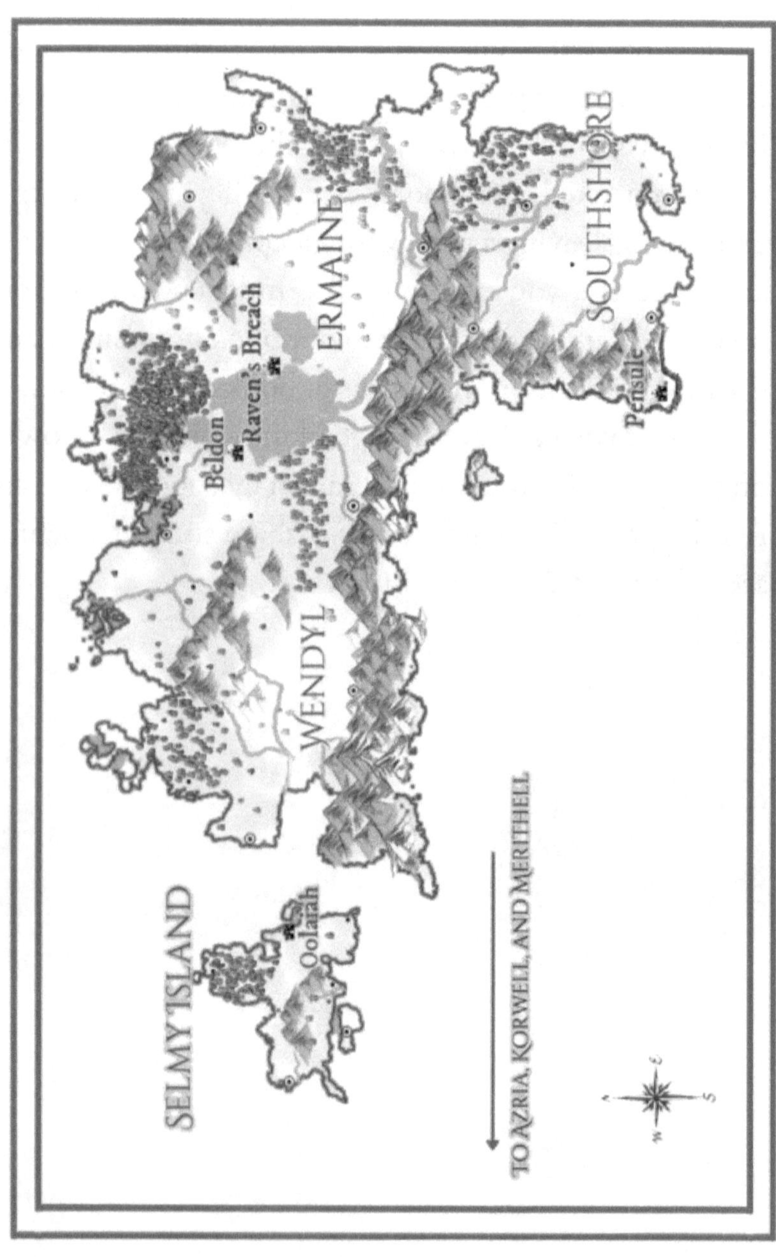
SOUTHSHORE
ERMAINE
Raven's Breach
Beldon
Pensile
WENDYL
SELMY ISLAND
Oolaah
TO AZRIA, KORWELL, AND MERITHELL
N
E
S
W

Don't miss out!

Visit the website below and you can sign up to receive emails whenever Mandi Richards publishes a new book. There's no charge and no obligation.

https://books2read.com/r/B-A-AGUP-BVARB

BOOKS 2 READ

Connecting independent readers to independent writers.

Also by Mandi Richards

Princesses of Selmy Island
Falcon's Kiss

Watch for more at mandirichards.com.

About the Author

Mandi Richards is the smut-writing alter of a good-girl nerd. She is first and foremost a mom of two wonderful boys and three kitties. She married her high school sweetheart, and she is an elementary school teacher. When she is not busy with all of that (which definitely doesn't leave her much time!) she can usually be found reading, playing dungeons and dragons, watching Disney princess movies and other musicals, or playing Minecraft.

Mandi always dreamed of being a Disney Princess, and when that did not pan out, she decided to invent her own princesses for grown-ups. She is currently focusing on her romantic fantasy trilogy featuring princesses and hot Fae with wings. This trilogy will be the start that introduces readers to her world that includes many other fantasy and fantasy romance tales waiting to be told.

Read more at mandirichards.com.